After the Fireworks

After the Fireworks

Aldous Huxley

ET REMOTISSIMA PROPE

Modern Voices

Modern Voices
Published by Hesperus Press Limited
4 Rickett Street, London SW6 1RU
www.hesperuspress.com

First published in *Brief Candles*, © 1930, renewed 1957 by Aldous Huxley
First published by Hesperus Press Limited, 2009

Foreword © Fay Weldon, 2009

Designed and typeset by Fraser Muggeridge studio
Printed in Jordan by Al-Khayyam Printing Press

ISBN: 978-1-84391-405-1

Contents

Foreword

For many years, Huxley (1894–1963), essayist, novelist, poet, and mystic, loomed – almost literally, he was 6 foot 4 inches tall – over the intellectual and aesthetic elite of this country. Other than as the author of the prophetic *Brave New World*, now seen as a companion piece to Orwell's *1984*, Huxley's reputation has waned as Orwell's has grown: he is no longer obligatory reading for the cultivated person. Perhaps this is because his declared aim as a writer of fiction was 'to arrive, technically, at a perfect fusion of the novel and the essay', and such an ambition will have done nothing to endear him to the touchy-feely, populist readers of the last few decades. But Huxley's time, I suspect, is coming again, as the age of empathy passes and the age of intellect reasserts itself. The publication of this novel by Hesperus Press suggests it is the case.

I first read *After the Fireworks* when I was eighteen, and it filled me with an uneasy fascination, mixed with shock and awe. I even remember where and when it was that I read it – the first Huxley novel I had come across. It was in the vaulted library of St Andrews University, in the winter of 1950, my red student gown wrapped around me for warmth, holding my breath with excitement as sentence piled on sentence, new idea on new idea. The erotic possibilities of the future dawned upon me. I had not anticipated life as being like this. I longed to be the 22-year-old Pamela of the novel, to seduce and be seduced by Fanning, the older, accomplished, discriminating man of letters, who knew which wine to choose, the significance of Etruscan art, how the world worked in general. Like Pamela I wanted to go 'down towards that mystical death, that apocalypse, that almost terrible transformation'.

It was a masochistic impulse, no doubt, but not surprising – back at a time when gender masochism was dinned into women and female graduates took shorthand-typing, and were grateful to end up as the secretary serving coffee to a high-powered boss. The Fanning/Pamela affair was bound to end in tears, I thought, closing the novel as the library closed; but never mind, the fireworks were spectacular. Indeed, the novel set me off on what was then seen as a wanton's path, though today such a path would be unremarkable enough. And today, of course, Pamela would not offer to do Fanning's ironing, in the absence of the household help. At least I hope not.

Rereading *After the Fireworks* now, understanding more, the fascination and the awe remains, though the shock of the new has gone. The book still disturbs – the sadomasochistic element is often there in Huxley's writing: the idea of the girl helpless in the face of a superior male and her own sexuality. But the sense of a piercing intelligence still leaps from the pages, and the exhilaration of ideas, the power of invention, and the adept handling of language still excites. In *After the Fireworks* we see not just Fanning and Pamela's tale, but something timeless, a dissection of lust, a picking to pieces of desire, as the cold blasts of reality and discomfort take their toll on unlikely lovers. It is a vision of the world in which the intellect itself is fired by sexual desire, a denial of centuries of thought in which sex was an expense of spirit in a waste of shame.

Huxley was privileged in his birth. He was a scion of the Huxley and Arnold families, who dominated the intellectual life of the mid and late Victorians, but no stranger to physical and emotional pain. Huxley's mother had died when he was fourteen – his housemaster at Eton cursorily breaking the news. He lost all but minimal sight from an untreated eye infection three years later and was to suffer headaches all his life; his beloved brother committed suicide. If he had – as they would say nowadays – 'issues', it is hardly surprising. *After the Fireworks* was written in 1929, shortly after the young (married) Huxley was recovering from a painful infatuation with the Paris Hilton of her day, the wild, rich and beautiful Nancy Cunard, a 'celebrity' before the word was invented.

No doubt the Huxley name opened literary doors for him. Aldous' father was Leonard Huxley the writer, his grandfather Thomas Huxley, the biologist: his mother Julia was a niece of Matthew Arnold and a sister of the novelist Mrs Humphrey Ward. (To have the name 'Huxley' was much the same as being a 'Freud' in today's society.) All the same, he had to support a family by writing from an early age, and it was no easier a matter then than it is now. His earlier novels – *Crome Yellow* in 1921, when he was twenty-six, then *Antic Hay, Those Barren Leaves* and *Point Counter Point* – came in such quick succession that he was lain open to the charge of being 'too prolific', that is, too facile for his own good. His extraordinary capacity to dissect the finer points of sexual desire, both male and female, saw him dismissed as 'cold-blooded and cynical' – not a good thing to be even in the callous twenties. But with the prescient *Brave New World*, in 1932, came acceptance and admiration.

The accusation of cynicism puzzled Huxley. He was not a cynical person, he protested: on the contrary. What he did was to try to discover the truth, and present it in fictional form. 'Facts do not cease to exist because they are ignored.' Or could it be, he asked others, that all that was nasty in him surfaced in his writing, rather than in himself?

In person Huxley was pleasing and persuasive enough. 'His six four seemed even taller because of the slenderness of his body and his slight stoop,' or so he is described in Sybille Bedford's admirable biography of the writer. 'Under the thick brown hair, his wide face was pale with full lips and blue eyes which had an inward look… he did not talk much at his first visit, but as soon as he was gone, everyone agreed about the deep impression of unique quality of gentleness and depth.'

In 1937 the Huxley family moved to California and Aldous tried his hand at screenwriting, not with great success, though in 1940 he got a credit for adapting *Pride and Prejudice,* and four years later for *Jane Eyre.* I have a fellow feeling with him here: half a century on, I adapted the former for television and the latter for stage. And also a kind of family feeling, inasmuch as my mother, a 'serious writer', obliged by financial circumstances to write for the market, as so many are, took to writing popular romances under the name Pearl Bellairs, which was the name Huxley chose for the egregious romantic novelist in his early short story *Farcical History of Richard Greenow.* They did very well indeed, but she lived in fear that Aldous or his heirs would one day discover and be furious.

Then, unexpectedly, Huxley's life and career moved off in another direction altogether. He experimented with mescalin, then the (quite legal) precursor of lysergic acid, better known as LSD. He came to see hallucinogens as the gateway to a greater human understanding and awareness, and with the publication of *The Perennial Philosophy* (1944), the essay collection *The Doors of Perception* (1954) and his final novel *Island* (1962), became the spiritual father, the guru, of the hippy movement – and, after a fashion, everything that has grown out of that since the sixties. This change in our consciousness, this cultural and epistemological mutation, this understanding of the shifting nature of reality, which dawned with the coming of psychedelic drugs, has left us with the world we have today. Blame – or happily attribute, according to temperament – our Gaian take on the planet, serious discussion of shakras, karmas and crystals, the end of gender role-playing, new theories of education, therapistic value systems, postmodern ethics, for our new awareness. Huxley did not, of course, create the new world on his own, but sitting there in the blazing Californian desert, thinking, writing as best he could with his bad eyes, that astonishing mind swirling with hallucinogenic visions, he set it on the path to now, for good or bad.

Early inklings of his future are here in *After the Fireworks*. Fanning, instructing Pamela on the subject of Homer as she stifles a yawn, comments that Shakespeare couldn't have written like that if he hadn't lived after the great split – 'the great split that broke life into spirit and matter, heroics and diabolics, virtue and sin and all the other accursed antitheses. Homer lived before the split.' It was this traditional split between the divine and the carnal that Huxley was always trying to heal, so that spirit and matter could become one thing, heroes be villains and villains heroes, virtue and sin hopelessly combined. No wonder the story unsettles. 'How right the Church has always been to persecute literature,' says Fanning. 'The harm we imaginative writers do! Enormous!'

– Fay Weldon, 2009

After the Fireworks

I

'Late as usual. Late.' Judd's voice was censorious. The words fell sharp, like beak-blows.

'As though I were a nut,' Miles Fanning thought resentfully, 'and he were a woodpecker. And yet he's devotion itself, he'd do anything for me. Which is why, I suppose, he feels entitled to crack my shell each time he sees me.' And he came to the conclusion, as he had so often come before, that he really didn't like Colin Judd at all.

'My oldest friend, whom I quite definitely don't like. Still...' Still, Judd was an asset, Judd was worth it.

'Here are your letters,' the sharp voice continued.

Fanning groaned as he took them.

'Can't one ever escape from letters? Even here, in Rome? They seem to get through everything. Like filter-passing bacteria. Those blessed days before post offices!'

Sipping, he examined, over the rim of his coffee cup, the addresses on the envelopes.

'You'd be the first to complain if people didn't write,' Judd rapped out. 'Here's your egg. Boiled for three minutes exactly. I saw to it myself.'

Taking his egg, 'On the contrary,' Fanning answered, 'I'd be the first to rejoice. If people write, it means they exist; and all I ask for is to be able to pretend that the world doesn't exist. The wicked flee when no man pursueth. How well I understand them! But letters don't allow you to be an ostrich. The Freudians say...' He broke off suddenly. After all, he was talking to Colin – to *Colin*. The confessional, self-accusatory manner was wholly misplaced. Pointless to give Colin the excuse to say something disagreeable. But what he had been going to say about the Freudians was amusing.

'The Freudians,' he began again. But taking advantage of forty years of intimacy, Judd had already started to be disagreeable.

'But you'd be miserable,' he was saying, 'if the post didn't bring you your regular dose of praise and admiration and sympathy and...'

'And humiliation,' added Fanning, who had opened one of the envelopes and was looking at the letter within.

'Listen to this. From my American publishers. Sales and Publicity Department. "My dear Mr Fanning." *My* dear, mark you. Wilbur F. Schmalz's dear. "My dear Mr Fanning, – Won't you take us into your confidence with regard to your plans for the Summer Vacation? What aspect of the Great Outdoors are you favouring this year? Ocean or Mountain, Woodland or purling Lake? I would esteem it a great privilege if you would inform me, as I am preparing a series of notes for the Literary Editors of our leading journals, who are, as I have often found in the past, exceedingly receptive to such personal material, particularly when accompanied by well-chosen snapshots. So won't you cooperate with us in providing this service? Very cordially yours, Wilbur F. Schmalz." Well, what do you think of that?'

'I think you'll answer him,' said Judd. 'Charmingly,' he added, envenoming his malice. Fanning gave a laugh, whose very ease and heartiness betrayed his discomfort. 'And you'll even send him a snapshot.'

Contemptuously – too contemptuously (he felt it at the time) – Fanning crumpled up the letter and threw it into the fireplace. The real humiliating thing, he reflected, was that Judd was quite right: he *would* write to Mr Schmalz about the Great Outdoors, he *would* send the first snapshot anybody took of him. There was a silence. Fanning ate two or three spoonfuls of egg. Perfectly boiled, for once. But still, what a relief that Colin was

4

going away! After all, he reflected, there's a great deal to be said for a friend who has a house in Rome and who invites you to stay, even when he isn't there. To such a man much must be forgiven – even his infernal habit of being a woodpecker. He opened another envelope and began to read.

Possessive and preoccupied, like an anxious mother, Judd watched him. With all his talents and intelligence, Miles wasn't fit to face the world alone. Judd had told him so (peck, peck!) again and again. 'You're a child!' He had said it a thousand times. 'You ought to have somebody to look after you.' But if anyone other than himself offered to do it, how bitterly jealous and resentful he became! And the trouble was that there were always so many applicants for the post of Fanning's bear-leader. Foolish men or, worse and more frequently, foolish women, attracted to him by his reputation and then conquered by his charm. Judd hated and professed to be loftily contemptuous of them. And the more Fanning liked his admiring bear-leaders, the loftier Judd's contempt became. For that was the bitter and unforgivable thing: Fanning manifestly preferred their bear-leading to Judd's. They flattered the bear, they caressed and even worshipped him; and the bear, of course, was charming to them, until such time as he growled, or bit, or, more often, quietly slunk away. Then they were surprised, they were pained. Because, as Judd would say with a grim satisfaction, they didn't know what Fanning was *really* like. Whereas he did know and had known since they were schoolboys together, nearly forty years before. Therefore he had a right to like him – a right and, at the same time, a duty to tell him all the reasons why he ought not to like him. Fanning didn't much enjoy listening to these reasons; he preferred to go where the bear was a sacred animal. With that air, which seemed so natural on his grey sharp face, of being dispassionately impersonal, 'You're afraid of healthy criticism,' Judd would tell him. 'You always were, even as a boy.'

5

'He's Jehovah,' Fanning would complain. 'Life with Judd is one long Old Testament. Being one of the Chosen People must have been bad enough. But to be *the* Chosen Person, in the singular...' And he would shake his head. 'Terrible!' And yet he had never seriously quarrelled with Colin Judd. Active unpleasantness was something which Fanning avoided as much as possible. He had never even made any determined attempt to fade out of Judd's existence as he had faded, at one time or another, out of the existence of so many once intimate bearleaders. The habit of their intimacy was of too long standing and, besides, old Colin was so useful, so bottomlessly reliable. So Judd remained for him the Oldest Friend whom one definitely dislikes; while for Judd, he was the Oldest Friend whom one adores and at the same time hates for not adoring back, the Oldest Friend whom one never sees enough of, but whom, when he *is* there, one finds insufferably exasperating, the Oldest Friend whom, in spite of all one's efforts, one is always getting on the nerves of.

'If only,' Judd was thinking, 'he could have faith!' The Catholic Church was there to help him. (Judd himself was a convert of more than twenty years' standing.) But the trouble was that Fanning didn't want to be helped by the Church; he could only see the comic side of Judd's religion. Judd was reserving his missionary efforts till his friend should be old or ill. But if only, meanwhile, if only, by some miracle of grace... So thought the good Catholic; but it was the jealous friend who felt and who obscurely schemed. Converted, Miles Fanning would be separated from his other friends and brought, Judd realised, nearer to himself.

Watching him, as he read his letter, Judd noticed, all at once, that Fanning's lips were twitching involuntarily into a smile. They were full lips, well cut, sensitive and sensual; his smiles were a little crooked. A dark fury suddenly fell on Colin Judd.

'Telling *me* that you'd like to get no letters!' he said with an icy vehemence. 'When you sit there grinning to yourself over some silly woman's flatteries.'

Amazed, amused, 'But what an outburst!' said Fanning, looking up from his letter.

Judd swallowed his rage; he had made a fool of himself. It was in a tone of calm dispassionate flatness that he spoke. Only his eyes remained angry.

'Was I right?' he asked.

'So far as the woman was concerned,' Fanning answered. 'But wrong about the flattery. Women have no time nowadays to talk about anything except themselves.'

'Which is only another way of flattering,' said Judd obstinately. 'They confide in you, because they think you'll like being treated as a person who understands.'

'Which is what, after all, I am. By profession even.' Fanning spoke with an exasperating mildness. 'What *is* a novelist, unless he's a person who understands?'

He paused; but Judd made no answer, for the only words he could have uttered would have been whirling words of rage and jealousy. He was jealous not only of the friends, the lovers, the admiring correspondents; he was jealous of a part of Fanning himself, of the artist, the public personage; for the artist, the public personage seemed so often to stand between his friend and himself. He hated, while he gloried in them.

Fanning looked at him for a moment, expectantly; but the other kept his mouth tight shut, his eyes averted. In the same exasperatingly gentle tone, 'And flattery or no flattery,' Fanning went on, 'this is a charming letter. And the girl's adorable.' He was having his revenge. Nothing upset poor Colin Judd so much as having to listen to talk about women or love. He had a horror of anything connected with the act, the mere thought, of sex. Fanning called it his perversion. 'You're one of those unspeakable chastity-perverts,' he would say, when he wanted to get his own back after a bout of pecking. 'If I had children, I'd never allow them to frequent your company. Too dangerous.' When he spoke of the forbidden subject, Judd would either writhe, a martyr, or else unchristianly explode. On this occasion he writhed and was silent. 'Adorable,' Fanning repeated, provocatively. 'A ravishing little creature. Though of course she *may* be a huge great camel. That's the danger of unknown correspondents. The best letter-writers are often camels. It's a piece of natural history I've learned by the bitterest experience.'

Looking back at the letter, 'All the same,' he went on, 'when a young girl writes to one that she's sure one's the only person in the world who can tell her exactly who and what (both heavily underlined) she is – well, one's rather tempted, I must confess, to try yet once more. Because even if she were a camel she'd be a very young one. Twenty-one – isn't that what she says?' He turned over a page of the letter. 'Yes; twenty-one. Also she writes in orange ink. And doesn't like the Botticellis at the Uffizi. But I hadn't told you; she's at Florence. This letter has been to London and back. We're practically neighbours. And here's something that's really rather good. Listen. "What I like about the Italian women is that they don't seem to be rather ashamed of being women, like so many English girls are, because English girls seem to go about apologising for their figures, as though they were punctured, the way they hold themselves – it's really rather abject. But here they're all pleased and proud and not a bit apologetic or punctured, but just the opposite, which I really like, don't you?" Yes, I do,' Fanning answered, looking up from the letter. 'I like it very much indeed. I've always been opposed to these modern *Ars est celare arsem*[1] fashions. I like unpuncturedness and I'm charmed by the letter. Yes, charmed. Aren't you?'

In a voice that trembled with hardly restrained indignation, 'No, I'm not!' Judd answered; and without looking at Fanning, he got up and walked quickly out of the room.

2

Judd had gone to stay with his old Aunt Caroline at Montreux. It was an annual affair; for Judd lived chronometrically. Most of June and the first half of July were always devoted to Aunt Caroline and devoted, invariably, at Montreux. On the fifteenth of July, Aunt Caroline was rejoined by her friend Miss Gaskin and Judd was free to proceed to England. In England he stayed till September the thirteenth, when he returned to Rome – 'for the praying season', as Fanning irreverently put it. The beautiful regularity of poor Colin's existence was a source of endless amusement to his friend. Fanning never had any plans.

'I just accept what turns up,' he would explain. 'Heads or tails – it's the only rational way of living. Chance generally knows so much better than we do. The Greeks elected most of their officials by lot – how wisely! Why shouldn't we toss up for Prime Ministers? We'd be much better governed. Or a sort of Calcutta Sweep for all the responsible posts in Church and State. The only horror would be if one were to win the sweep oneself. Imagine drawing the Permanent Under-Secretaryship for Education! Or the Archbishopric of Canterbury! Or the Viceroyalty of India! One would just have to drink weed-killer. But as things are, luckily…'

Luckily, he was at liberty, under the present dispensation, to stroll, very slowly, in a suit of cream-coloured silk, down the shady side of the via Condotti towards the Spanish Steps. Slowly, slowly. The air was streaked with invisible bars of heat and cold. Coolness came flowing out of shadowed doorways, and at every transverse street the sun breathed fiercely. Like walking through the ghost of a zebra, he thought.

Three beautiful young women passed him, talking and laughing together. Like laughing flowers, like deer, like little horses. And of course absolutely unpunctured, unapologetic, he smiled to himself, thinking of the letter and also of his own reply to it.

A pair of pink and white monsters loomed up, as though from behind the glass of an aquarium. But not speechless. For *'Großartig!'*[2] fell enthusiastically on Fanning's ear as they passed, and *'Fabelhaft!'*[3] These Nordics! He shook his head. Time they were put a stop to.

In the looking-glasses of a milliner's window a tall man in creamy-white walked slowly to meet him, hat in hand. The face was aquiline and eager, brown with much exposure to the sun. The waved, rather wiry hair was dark almost to blackness. It grew thickly, and the height of the forehead owed nothing to the approach of baldness. But what pleased Fanning most was the slimness and straightness of the tall figure. Those sedentary men of letters, with their sagging tremulous paunches – they were enough to make one hate the very thought of literature. What had been Fanning's horror when, a year before, he had realised that his own paunch was showing the first preliminary signs of sagging! But Mr Hornibrooke's exercises had been wonderful. 'The Culture of the Abdomen.' So much more important, as he had remarked in the course of the last few months at so many dinner tables, than the culture of the mind! For of course he had taken everybody into his confidence about the paunch. He took everybody into his confidence about almost everything. About his love affairs and his literary projects; about his illnesses and his philosophy; his vices and his bank balance. He lived a rich and variegated private life in public; it was one of the secrets of his charm.

To the indignant protests of poor jealous Colin, who reproached him with being an exhibitionist, shameless, a self-exploiter, 'You take everything so moralistically,' he had answered. 'You seem to imagine people do everything on purpose. But people do hardly anything on purpose. They behave as they do because they can't help it; that's what they happen to be like. "I am that I am"; Jehovah's is the last word in realistic psychology. I am what *I* am – a sort of soft transparent jellyfish. While you're what *you* are – very tightly shut, opaque, heavily armoured: in a word, a giant clam. Morality doesn't enter; it's a case for scientific classification. You should be more of a Linnaeus, Colin, and less the Samuel Smiles.'

Judd had been reduced to a grumbling silence. What he really resented was the fact that Fanning's confidences were given to upstart friends, to strangers even, before they were given to him. It was only to be expected. The clam's shell keeps the outside things out as effactually as it keeps the inside things in. In Judd's case, moreover, the shell served as an instrument of reproachful pinching.

From his cool street Fanning emerged into the Piazza di Spagna. The sunlight was stinging hot and dazzling. The flower vendors on the steps sat in the midst of great explosions of colour. He bought a gardenia from one of them and stuck it in his buttonhole. From the windows of the English bookshop 'The Return of Eurydice, by Miles Fanning' stared at him again and again. They were making a regular display of his latest volume in Tauchnitz. Satisfactory, no doubt; but also, of course, rather ridiculous and even humiliating, when one reflected that the book would be read by people like that estimable upper middle-class couple there, with their noses at the next window – that Civil Servant, he guessed, with the sweet little artistic wife and the artistic little house on Campden Hill – would be read by them dutifully (for of course they worked hard to keep abreast of everything) and discussed at their charming little dinner parties and finally condemned as 'extraordinarily brilliant, but...' Yes, but, but, but. For they were obviously regular subscribers to *Punch,* were vertebrae in the backbone of England, were upholders of all that was depressingly finest, all that was lifelessly and genteelly best in the English upper-class tradition. And when they recognised him (as it was obvious to Fanning, in spite of their discreet politeness, that they did) his vanity, instead of being flattered, was hurt. Being recognised by people like that – such was fame! What a humiliation, what a personal insult!

At Cook's, where he now went to draw some money on his letter of credit, Fame still pursued him, trumpeting. From behind the brass bars of his cage the cashier smiled knowingly as he counted the banknotes.

'Of course your name's very familiar to me, Mr Fanning,' he said; and his tone was at once ingratiating and self-satisfied; the compliment to Fanning was at the same time a compliment to himself. 'And if I may be permitted to say so,' he went on, pushing the money through the bars, as one might offer a piece of bread to an ape, 'gratters on your last book. Gratters,' he repeated, evidently delighted with his very public-schooly colloquialism.

'All gratitude for gratters,' Fanning answered and turned away.

He was half amused, half annoyed. Amused by the absurdity of those more than Etonian congratulations, annoyed at the damned impertinence of the congratulator. 'So intolerably patronising!' he grumbled to himself. But most admirers were like that; they thought they were doing you an enormous favour by admiring you. And how much more they admired themselves for being capable of appreciating than they admired the object of their appreciation! And then there were the earnest ones who thanked you for giving such a perfect expressions to their ideas and sentiments. They were the worst of all. For, after all, what were they thanking you for? For being *their* interpreter, *their* dragoman, for playing John the Baptist to *their* Messiah. Damn their impertinence! Yes, damn their impertinence!

'Mr Fanning.' A hand touched his elbow.

Still indignant with the thought of damned impertinences, Fanning turned round with an expression of such ferocity on his face that the young woman who had addressed him involuntarily fell back.

'Oh... I'm so sorry,' she stammered; and her face, which had been bright, deliberately, with just such an impertinence as Fanning was damning, was discomposed into a child-like embarrassment. The blood tingled painfully in her cheeks. Oh, what a fool, she thought, what a fool she was making of herself! This idiotic blushing! But the way he had turned round on her, as if he were going to bite... Still, even that was no excuse for blushing and saying she was sorry, as though she were still at school and he were Miss Huss. Idiot! she inwardly shouted at herself. And making an enormous effort, she readjusted her still scarlet face, giving it as good an expression of smiling nonchalance as she could summon up. 'I'm sorry,' she repeated, in a voice that was meant to be light, easy, ironically polite, but which came out (oh, idiot, idiot!) nervously shaky and uneven.

'I'm afraid I disturbed you. But I just wanted to introduce... I mean, as you were passing...'

'But how charming of you!' said Fanning, who had had time to realise that this latest piece of impertinence was one to be blessed, not damned. 'Charming!'

Yes, charming it was, that young face with the grey eyes and the little straight nose, like a cat's, and the rather short upper lip. And the heroic way she had tried, through all her blushes, to be the accomplished woman of the world – that too was charming. And touchingly charming even were those rather red, large-wristed English hands, which she wasn't yet old enough to have learnt the importance of tending into whiteness and softness. They were still the hands of a child, a tomboy. He gave her one of those quick, those brilliantly and yet mysteriously significant smiles of his; those smiles that were still so youth-fully beautiful when they came spontaneously. But they could also be put on; he knew how to exploit their fabricated charm, deliberately. To a sensitive eye, the beauty of his expression was, on these occasions, subtly repulsive.

Reassured, 'I'm Pamela Tarn,' said the young girl, feeling warm with gratitude for the smile. He was handsomer, she was thinking, than in his photographs. And much more fascinating. It was a face that had to be seen in movement.

'Pamela Tarn?' he repeated questioningly.

'The one who wrote you a letter.' Her blush began to deepen again. 'You answered so nicely. I mean, it was so kind… I thought…'

'But of course!' he cried, so loudly that people looked round, startled. 'Of course!'

He took her hand and held it, shaking it from time to time, for what seemed to Pamela hours.

'The most enchanting letter. Only I'm so bad at names. So you're Pamela Tarn.'

He looked at her appraisingly. She returned his look for a moment, then flinched away in confusion from his bright dark eyes.

'Excuse me,' said a chilly voice; and a very large suit of plus-fours edged past them to the door.

'I like you,' Fanning concluded, ignoring the plus-fours; she uttered an embarrassed little laugh. 'But then, I liked you before. You don't know how pleased I was with what you said about the difference between English and Italian women.'

The colour rose once more into Pamela's cheeks. She had only written those sentences after long hesitation, and had written them recklessly, dashing them down with a kind of anger, just because Miss Huss would have been horrified by their unwo-manliness, just because Aunt Edith would have found them so distressing, just because they had, when she spoke them aloud one day in the streets of Florence, so shocked the two school-mistresses from Boston whom she had met at the pension and was doing the sights with. Fanning's mention of them pleased her and at the same time made her feel dreadfully guilty. She hoped he wouldn't be too specific about those differences; it seemed to her that everyone was listening.

'So profound,' he went on in his musical ringing voice. 'But out of the mouths of babes, with all due respect.' He smiled again, 'And "punctured" – that was really the *mot juste*. I shall steal it and use it as my own.'

'*Permesso*.' This time it was a spotted muslin and brown arms and a whiff of synthetic carnations.

'I think we're rather in the way,' said Pamela, who was becoming more and more uncomfortably aware of being conspicuous.

And the spirit presences of Miss Huss, of Aunt Edith, of the two American ladies at Florence seemed to hang about her, hauntingly.

'Perhaps we'd better… I mean…' And, turning, she almost ran to the door.

'Punctured, punctured,' repeated his pursuing voice behind her. 'Punctured with the shame of being warm-blooded mammals. Like those poor lank creatures that were standing at the counter in there,' he added, coming abreast with her, as they stepped over the threshold into the heat and glare. 'Did you see them? So pathetic. But, oh dear!' he shook his head. 'Oh dear, oh dear!'

She looked up at him, and Fanning saw in her face a new expression, an expression of mischief and laughing malice and youthful impertinence. Even her breasts, he now noticed with an amused appreciation, even her breasts were impertinent. Small, but beneath the pale blue stuff of her dress, pointed, firm, almost comically insistent. No ashamed deflation here.

'Pathetic,' she mockingly echoed, 'but, oh dear, how horrible, how disgusting! Because they *are* disgusting,' she added defiantly, in answer to his look of humorous protest. Here in the sunlight and with the noise of the town isolating her from everyone except Fanning, she had lost her embarrassment and her sense of guilt. The spiritual presences had evaporated. Pamela was annoyed with herself for having felt so uncomfortable among those awful old English cats at Cook's. She thought of her mother; her mother had never been embarrassed, or at any rate she had always managed to turn her embarrassment into something else. Which was what Pamela was doing now.

'Really disgusting,' she almost truculently insisted. She was reasserting herself, she was taking a revenge.

'You're very ruthless to the poor old things,' said Fanning. 'So worthy in spite of their mangy dimness, so obviously good.'

'I hate goodness,' said Pamela with decision, speeding the parting ghosts of Miss Huss and Aunt Edith and the two ladies from Boston.

Fanning laughed aloud. 'Ah, if only we all had the courage to say so, like you, my child!' And with a familiar affectionate gesture, as though she were indeed a child and he had known her from the cradle, he dropped a hand on her shoulder. 'To say so and to act up to our beliefs. As you do, I'm sure.' And he gave the slim hard shoulder a pat. 'A world without goodness – it'd be Paradise.'

They walked some steps in silence. His hand lay heavy and strong on her shoulder, and a strange warmth that was somehow intenser than the warmth of mere flesh and blood seemed to radiate through her whole body. Her heart quickened its beating; an anxiety oppressed her lungs; her very mind was as though breathless.

'Putting his hand on my shoulder like that!' she was thinking. 'It would have been cheek if someone else... Perhaps I ought to have been angry, perhaps...' No, that would have been silly. 'It's silly to take things like that too seriously, as though one were Aunt Edith.' But meanwhile his hand lay heavy on her shoulder, broodingly hot, its weight, its warmth insistently present in her consciousness.

She remembered characters in his books. Her namesake Pamela in *Pastures New*. Pamela the cold, but for that very reason an experimenter with passion; cold and therefore dangerous, full of power, fatal. Was she like Pamela? She had often thought so. But more recently she had often thought she was like Joan in *The Return of Eurydice* – Joan, who had emerged from the wintry dark underworld of an unawakened life with her husband (that awful, good, disinterested husband – so like Aunt Edith) into the warmth and brilliance of that transfiguring passion for Walter, for the adorable Walter whom she had always imagined must be so like Miles Fanning himself. She was sure of it now. But what of her own identity? Was she Joan, or was she Pamela? And which of the two would it be nicer to be? Warm Joan, with her happiness – but at the price of surrender? Or the cold, the unhappy, but conquering, dangerous Pamela? Or wouldn't it perhaps be best to be a little of both at once? Or first one and then the other? And in any case there was to be no goodness in the Aunt Edith style; he had been sure she wasn't good.

In her memory the voice of Aunt Edith sounded, as it had actually sounded only a few weeks before, in disapproving comment on her reference to the passionless, experimental Pamela of *Pastures New*.

'It's a book I don't like. A most unnecessary book.' And then, laying her hand on Pamela's, 'Dear child,' she had added, with that earnest, that dutifully willed affectionateness, which Pamela so bitterly resented, 'I'd rather you didn't read any of Miles Fanning's books.'

'Mother never objected to my reading them. So I don't see…' The triumphant consciousness of having at this very moment the hand that had written those unnecessary books upon her shoulder was promising to enrich her share of the remembered dialogue with a lofty impertinence which the original had hardly possessed. 'I don't see that you have the smallest right…'

Fanning's voice fell startlingly across the eloquent silence. 'A penny for your thoughts, Miss Pamela,' it said.

He had been for some obscure reason suddenly depressed by his own last words. 'A world without goodness – it'd be Paradise.' But it wouldn't, no more than now. The only paradises were fools' paradises, ostriches' paradises. It was as though he had suddenly lifted his head out of the sand and seen time bleeding away – like the stabbed bull at the end of a bull-fight, swaying on his legs and soundlessly spouting the red blood from his nostrils – bleeding, bleeding stanchlessly into the darkness. And it was all, even the loveliness and the laughter and the sunlight, finally pointless. This young girl at his side, this beautiful pointless creature pointlessly walking down the via del Babuino… The feelings crystallised themselves, as usual, into whole phrases in his mind, and suddenly the phrases were metrical.

Pointless and arm in arm with pointlessness,
I pace and pace the Street of the Baboon.

Imbecile! Annoyed with himself, he tried to shake off his mood of maudlin depression, he tried to force his spirit back into the ridiculous and charming universe it had inhabited, on the whole so happily, all the morning.

'A penny for your thoughts,' he said, with a certain rather forced jocularity, giving her shoulder a little clap. 'Or forty centesimi, if you prefer them.' And, dropping his hand to his side, 'In Germany,' he went on, 'just after the war one could afford to be more munificent. There was a time when I regularly offered a hundred and ninety million marks for a thought – yes, and gained on the exchange. But now...'

'Well, if you really want to know,' said Pamela, deciding to be bold, 'I was thinking how much my Aunt Edith disapproved of your books.'

'Did she? I suppose it was only to be expected. Seeing that I don't write for aunts – at any rate, not for aunts in their specifically auntly capacity. Though, of course, when they're off duty...'

'Aunt Edith's never off duty.'

'And I'm never on. So you see.' He shrugged his shoulders. 'But I'm sure,' he added, 'you never paid much attention to her disapproval.'

'None,' she answered, playing the un-good part for all it was worth. 'I read Freud this spring,' she boasted, 'and Gide's autobiography, and Krafft-Ebbing...'

'Which is more than I've ever done,' he laughed.

The laugh encouraged her. 'Not to mention all *your* books, years ago. You see,' she added, suddenly fearful lest she might have said something to offend him, 'my mother never minded me reading your books. I mean, she really encouraged me, even when I was only seventeen or eighteen. My mother died last year,' she explained. There was a silence. 'I've lived with Aunt Edith ever since,' she went on. 'Aunt Edith's my father's sister. Older than he was. Father died in 1923.'

'So you're all alone now?' he questioned. 'Except, of course, for Aunt Edith.'

'Whom I've now left.' She was almost boasting again. 'Because when I was twenty-one...'

'You stuck out your tongue at her and ran away. Poor Aunt Edith!

'I won't have you being sorry for her,' Pamela answered hotly. 'She's really awful, you know. Like poor Joan's husband in *The Return of Eurydice*.' How easy it was to talk to him!

'So you even know,' said Fanning, laughing, 'what it's like to be unhappily married. Already. Indissolubly wedded to a virtuous aunt.'

'No joke, I can tell you. *I'm* the one to be sorry for. Besides, she didn't mind my going away, whatever she might say.'

'She did say something, then?'

'Oh yes. She always says things. More in sorrow than in anger, you know. Like headmistresses. So gentle and good, I mean. When all the time she really thought me too awful. I used to call her Hippo, because she was such a hypocrite – *and* so fat. Enormous. Don't you *hate* enormous people? No, she's really delighted to get rid of me,' Pamela concluded, 'simply delighted.'

Her face was flushed and as though luminously alive; she spoke with a quick eagerness.

'What a tremendous hurry she's in,' he was thinking, 'to tell me all about herself. If she were older or uglier, what an intolerable egotism it would be! As intolerable as mine would be if I happened to be less intelligent. But as it is…' His face, as he listened to her, expressed a sympathetic attention.

'She always disliked me,' Pamela had gone on. 'Mother too. She couldn't abide my mother, though she was always sweetly hippo-ish with her.'

'And your mother – how did she respond?'

'Well, not hippo-ishly, of course. She couldn't be that. She treated Aunt Edith – well, how *did* she treat Aunt Edith?' Pamela hesitated, frowning. 'Well, I suppose you'd say she was just natural with the Hippo. I mean…' She bit her lip. 'Well, if she ever *was* really natural. *I* don't know. Is anybody natural?' She looked up questioningly at Fanning. 'Am I natural, for example?'

Smiling a little at her choice of an example, 'I should think almost certainly not,' Fanning answered, more or less at random.

'You're right, of course,' she said despairingly, and her face was suddenly tragic, almost there were tears in her eyes. 'But isn't it awful? I mean, isn't it simply hopeless?'

Pleased that his chance shot should have gone home, 'At your age,' he said consolingly, 'you can hardly expect to be natural. Naturalness is something you learn, painfully, by trial and error. Besides,' he added, 'there are some people who are unnatural by nature.'

'Unnatural by nature.' Pamela nodded, as she repeated the words, as though she were inwardly marshalling evidence to confirm their truth. 'Yes, I believe that's us,' she concluded. 'Mother and me. Not hippos, I mean, not *poseuses*, but just unnatural by nature. You're quite right. As usual,' she added, with something that was almost resentment in her voice.

'I'm sorry,' he apologised.

'How is it you manage to know so much?' Pamela asked in the same resentful tone. By what right was he so easily omniscient, when she could only grope and guess in the dark?

Taking to himself a credit that belonged, in this case, to chance, 'Child's play, my dear Watson,' he answered banteringly. 'But I suppose you're too young to have heard of Sherlock Holmes. And anyhow,' he added, with an ironical seriousness, 'don't let's waste any more time talking about me.'

Pamela wasted no more time.

'I get so depressed with myself,' she said with a sigh. 'And after what you've told me I shall get more depressed. Unnatural by nature. And by upbringing too. Because I see now that my mother was like that. I mean, she was unnatural by nature too.'

'Even with you?' he asked, thinking that this was becoming interesting. She nodded without speaking. He looked at her closely. 'Were you very fond of her?' was the question that now suggested itself.

After a moment of silence, 'I loved my father more,' she answered slowly. 'He was more... more reliable. I mean, you never quite knew where you were with my mother. Sometimes she almost forgot about me; or else she didn't forget me enough and spoiled me. And then sometimes she used to get into the most terrible rages with me. She really frightened me then. And said such terribly hurting things. But you mustn't think I didn't love her. I did.'

The words seemed to release a spring; she was suddenly moved. There was a little silence.

Making an effort, 'But that's what she was like,' she concluded at last.

'But I don't see,' said Fanning gently, 'that there was anything specially unnatural in spoiling you and then getting cross with you.' They were crossing the Piazza del Popolo; the traffic of four thronged streets intricately merged and parted in the open space. 'You must have been a charming child. And also... Look out!' He laid a hand on her arm. An electric bus passed noiselessly, a whispering monster. 'Also maddeningly exasperating. So where the unnaturalness came in...'

'But if you'd known her,' Pamela interrupted, 'you'd have seen exactly where the unnaturalness...'

'Forward!' he called and, still holding her arm, he steered her on across the Piazza.

She suffered herself to be conducted blindly. 'It came out in the way she spoiled me,' she explained, raising her voice against the clatter of a passing lorry. 'It's so difficult to explain, though; because it's something I felt. I mean, I've never really tried to put it into words till now. But it was as if... as if she weren't just herself spoiling me, but the picture of a young mother – do you see what I mean? – spoiling the picture of a young girl. Even as a child I kind of felt it wasn't quite as it should be. Later on I began to *know* it too, here.'

She tapped her forehead. 'Particularly after father's death, when I was beginning to grow up. There were times when it was almost like listening to recitations – dreadful. One feels so blushy and prickly; you know the feeling.'

He nodded. 'Yes, I know. Awful!'

'Awful,' she repeated. 'So you can understand what a beast I felt, when it took me that way. So disloyal, I mean. So ungrateful. Because she was being so wonderfully sweet to me. You've no idea. But it was just when she was being her sweetest that I got the feeling worst. I shall never forget when she made me call her Clare – that was her Christian name. "Because we're going to be companions," she said, and all that sort of thing. Which was simply too sweet and too nice of her. But if you'd heard the way she said it! So dreadfully unnatural. I mean, it was almost as bad as Aunt Edith reading *Prospice*. And yet I know she meant it, I know she wanted me to be her companion. But somehow something kind of went wrong on the way between the wanting and the saying. And then the doing seemed to go just as wrong as the saying. She always wanted to do things excitingly, romantically, like in a play. But you can't *make* things be exciting and romantic, can you?'

Fanning shook his head.

'She wanted to kind of force things to be thrilling by thinking and wishing, like Christian Science. But it doesn't work. We had wonderful times together; but she always tried to make out that they were more wonderful than they really were. Which only made them less wonderful. Going to the Paris Opera on a gala night is wonderful; but it's never as wonderful as when Rastignac goes, is it?'

'I should think it wasn't!' he agreed. 'What an insult to Balzac to imagine that it could be!'

'And the real thing's less wonderful,' she went on, 'when you're being asked all the time to see it as Balzac, and to *be* Balzac yourself. When you aren't anything of the kind. Because, after all, what am I? Just good, ordinary, middle-class English.'

She pronounced the words with a kind of defiance. Fanning imagined that the defiance was for him and, laughing, prepared to pick up the ridiculous little glove. But the glove was not for him; Pamela had thrown it down to a memory, to a ghost, to one of her own sceptical and mocking selves. It had been on the last day of their last stay together in Paris – that exciting, exotic Paris of poor Clare's imagination, to which their tickets from London never seemed quite to take them. They had gone to lunch at La Pérouse.

'Such a marvellous, *fantastic* restaurant! It makes you feel as though you were back in the Second Empire.' (Or was it the First Empire? Pamela could not exactly remember.)

The rooms were so crowded with Americans that it was with some difficulty that they secured a table.

'We'll have a marvellous lunch,' Clare had said, as she unfolded her napkin. 'And some day, when you're in Paris with your lover, you'll come here and order just the same things as we're having today. And perhaps you'll think of me. Will you, darling?'

And she had smiled at her daughter with that intense, expectant expression that was so often on her face, and the very memory of which made Pamela feel subtly uncomfortable.

'How should I ever forget?' she had answered, laying her hand on her mother's and smiling.

But after a second her eyes had wavered away from that fixed look, in which the intensity had remained as desperately on the stretch, the expectancy as wholly unsatisfied, as hungrily insatiable as ever. The waiter, thank goodness, had created a timely diversion; smiling at him confidentially, almost amorously, Clare had ordered like a princess in a novel of high life. The bill, when it came, was enormous. Clare had had to scratch the bottom of her purse for the last stray piece of nickel.

'It looks as though we shall have to carry our own bags at Calais and Dover. I didn't realise I'd run things so fine.'

Pamela had looked at the bill.

'But, Clare,' she had protested, looking up again at her mother with an expression of genuine horror, 'it's wicked! Two hundred and sixty francs for a lunch! It wasn't worth it.'

The blood had risen darkly into Clare's face.

'How can you be so disgustingly *bourgeoise*, Pamela? So crass, so crawling?'

Incensed by the heaping up of this abuse, 'I think it's stupid to do things one can't afford,' the girl had answered; 'stupid and vulgar.'

Trembling with rage, Clare had risen to her feet. 'I'll never take you out again. Never.' (How often since then Pamela had recalled that terribly prophetic word!) 'You'll never understand life, you'll never be anything but a sordid little middle-class Englishwoman. Never, never.'

And she had swept out of the room, like an insulted queen.

Overheard by Pamela, as she undignifiedly followed, 'Gee!' an American voice had remarked, 'it's a regular cat-fight.'

The sound of another, real voice overlaid the remembered Middle Western accents. 'But after all,' Fanning was saying, 'it's better to be a good ordinary bourgeois than a bad ordinary bohemian, or a sham aristocrat, or a second-rate individual…'

'I'm not even third-rate,' said Pamela mournfully. There had been a time when, under the influence of the now abhorred Miss Huss, she had thought she would like to go up to Oxford and read Greats. But Greek grammar was so awful… 'Not even fourth-rate.'

'Thank goodness,' said Fanning. 'Do you know what third and fourth-rate intellectuals are? They're professors of philology and organic chemistry at the minor universities, they're founders and honorary life presidents of the Nuneaton Poetry Society and the Baron's Court Debating Society; they're the people who organise and sedulously attend all those conferences for promoting international goodwill and the spread of culture that are perpetually held at Budapest and Prague and Stockholm. Admirable and indispensable creatures, of course! But impossibly dreary; one simply cannot have any relations with them. And how virtuously they disapprove of those of us who have something better to do than disseminate culture or foster goodwill – those of us who are concerned, for example, with creating beauty – like me; or, like you, my child, in deliciously *being* beauty.'

Pamela blushed with pleasure, and for that reason felt it necessary immediately to protest.

'All the same,' she said, 'it's rather humiliating not to be able to do anything but be. I mean, even a cow can be.'

'Damned well, too,' said Fanning. 'If I *were* as intensely as a cow *is*, I'd be uncommonly pleased with myself. But this is getting almost too metaphysical. And do you realise what the time is?'

He held out his watch; it was ten past one.

'And where are we? At the Tiber. We've walked miles.' He waved his hand; a passing taxi swerved in to the pavement beside them. 'Let's go and eat some lunch. You're free?'

'Well...' She hesitated. It was marvellous, of course; so marvellous that she felt she ought to refuse. 'If I'm not a bore. I mean, I don't want to impose... I mean...'

'You mean you'll come and have lunch. Good. Do you like marble halls and bands? Or local colour?'

Pamela hesitated. She remembered her mother once saying that Valadier and the Ulpia were the *only* two restaurants in Rome.

'Personally,' Fanning went on, 'I'm slightly avaricious about marble halls. I rather resent spending four times as much as eating about two-thirds as well. But I'll overcome my avarice if you prefer them.'

Pamela duly voted for local colour; he gave an address to the driver and they climbed into the cab.

'It's a genuinely Roman place,' Fanning explained. 'I hope you'll like it.'

'Oh, I'm sure I shall.' All the same, she did rather wish they were going to Valadier's.

3

Fanning's old friend, Dodo del Grillo, was in Rome for that one night and had urgently summoned him to dine. His arrival was loud and exclamatory.

'Best of all possible Dodos!' he cried, as he advanced with outstretched hands across the enormous baroque saloon. 'What an age! But what a pleasure!'

'At last, Miles,' she said reproachfully; he was twenty minutes late.

'But I know you'll forgive me.' And laying his two hands on her shoulders he bent down and kissed her. He made a habit of kissing all his women friends.

'And even if I didn't forgive, you wouldn't care two pins.'

'Not one.' He smiled his most charming smile. 'But if it gives you the smallest pleasure, I'm ready to say I'd be inconsolable.' His hands still resting on her shoulders, he looked at her searchingly, at arm's length. 'Younger than ever,' he concluded.

'I couldn't look as young as you do,' she answered. 'You know, Miles, you're positively indecent. Like Dorian Gray. What's your horrible secret?'

'Simply Mr Hornibrooke,' he explained. 'The culture of the abdomen. So much more important than the culture of the mind.'

Dodo only faintly smiled; she had heard the joke before. Fanning was sensitive to smiles; he changed the subject.

'And where's the marquis?' he asked.

The marchesa shrugged her shoulders. Her husband was one of those dear old friends whom somehow one doesn't manage to see anything of nowadays.

'Filippo's in Tanganyika,' she explained. 'Hunting lions.'

'While you hunt them at home. And with what success! You've bagged what's probably the finest specimen in Europe this evening. Congratulations!'

'*Merci, cher maître!*' she laughed. 'Shall we go in to dinner?'

The words invited, irresistibly. 'If only I had the right to answer, *Oui, Chère maîtresse!*'

Though as a matter of fact, he reflected, he had never really found her at all interesting in that way. A woman without temperament. But very pretty once – that time (how many years ago?) when there had been that picnic on the river at Bray, and he had drunk a little too much champagne.

'If only!' he repeated; and then was suddenly struck by a grotesque thought. Suppose she were to say yes, now – now! 'If only I had the right!'

'But luckily,' said Dodo, turning back towards him, as she passed through the monumental door into the dining room, 'luckily you haven't the right. You ought to congratulate me on my immense good sense. Will you sit there?'

'Oh, I'll congratulate. I'm always ready to congratulate people who have sense.' He unfolded his napkin. 'And to condole.' Now that he knew himself safe, he could condole as much as he liked. 'What you must have suffered, my poor sensible Dodo, what you must have missed!'

'Suffered less,' she answered, 'and missed more unpleasantness than the women who didn't have the sense to say no.'

'What a mouthful of negatives! But that's how sensible people always talk about love – in terms of negatives. Never of positives; they ignore those and go about sensibly avoiding the discomforts. Avoiding the pleasures and exultations too, poor sensible idiots! Avoiding all that's valuable and significant. But it's always like that. The human soul is a fried whiting. (What excellent red mullet this is, by the way! Really excellent.) Its tail is in its mouth. All progress finally leads back to the beginning again. The most sensible people – dearest Dodo, believe me – are the most foolish. The most intellectual are the stupidest. I've never met a really good metaphysician, for example, who wasn't in one way or another bottomlessly stupid. And as for the really spiritual people, look what they revert to. Not merely to silliness and stupidity, but finally to crass non-existence. The highest spiritual state is ecstasy, which is just not being there at all. No, no; we're all fried whitings. Heads are invariably tails.'

'In which case,' said Dodo, 'tails must also be heads. So that if you want to make intellectual or spiritual progress, you must behave like a beast – is that it?'

Fanning held up his hand. 'Not at all. If you rush too violently towards the tail, you run the risk of shooting down the whiting's open mouth into its stomach, and even further. The wise man...'

'So the whitings are fried without being cleaned?'

'In parables,' Fanning answered reprovingly, 'whitings are always fried that way. The wise man, as I was saying, oscillates lightly from head to tail and back again. His whole existence – or shall we be more frank and say "my" whole existence? – is one continual oscillation. I am never too consistently sensible, like you; or too consistently feather-headed like some of my other friends. In a word,' he wagged a finger, 'I oscillate.'

Tired of generalisations, 'And where exactly,' Dodo enquired, 'have you oscillated to at the moment? You've left me without your news so long...'

'Well, at the moment,' he reflected aloud, 'I suppose you might say I was at a dead point between desire and renunciation, between sense and sensuality.'

'Again?' She shook her head. 'And who is she this time?'

Fanning helped himself to asparagus before replying. 'Who is she?' he echoed. 'Well, to begin with, she's the writer of admiring letters.'

Dodo made a grimace of disgust. 'What a horror!' For some reason she felt it necessary to be rather venomous about this new usurper of Fanning's heart. 'Vamping by correspondence – it's really the lowest...'

'Oh, I agree,' he said. 'On principle and in theory I entirely agree.'

'Then why…' she began, annoyed by his agreement; but he interrupted her.

'Spiritual adventuresses,' he said. 'That's what they generally are, the women who write you letters. Spiritual adventuresses. I've suffered a lot from them in my time.'

'I'm sure you have.'

'They're a curious type,' he went on, ignoring her sarcasms. 'Curious and rather horrible. I prefer the good old-fashioned vampire. At least one knew where one stood with her. There she was – out for money, for power, for a good time, occasionally, perhaps, for sensual satisfactions. It was all entirely aboveboard and obvious. But with the spiritual adventuress, on the contrary, everything's most horribly turbid and obscure and slimy. You see, she doesn't want money or the commonplace good time. She wants Higher Things – damn her neck! Not large pearls and a large motor car, but a large soul – that's what she pines for: a large soul and a large intellect, and a huge philosophy, and enormous culture, and outsizes in great thoughts.'

Dodo laughed. 'You're fiendishly cruel, Miles.'

'Cruelty can be a sacred duty,' he answered. 'Besides, I'm getting a little of my own back. If you knew what these spiritual vamps had done to me! I've been one of their appointed victims. Yes, appointed; for, you see, they can't have their Higher Things without attaching themselves to a Higher Person.'

'And are you one of the Higher People, Miles?'

'Should I be dining here with you, my dear, if I weren't?' And without waiting for Dodo's answer, 'They attach themselves like lice,' he went on. 'The contact with the Higher Person makes them feel high themselves; it magnifies them, it gives them significance, it satisfies their parasitic will to power. In the past they could have gone to religion – fastened themselves on the nearest priest (that's what the priest was there for), or sucked the spiritual blood of some saint. Nowadays they've got no professional victims; only a few charlatans and swamis and higher-thought-mongers. Or alternatively the artists. Yes, the artists. They find our souls particularly juicy. What I've suffered! Shall I ever forget that American woman who got so excited by my book on Blake that she came specially to Tunis to see me? She had an awful way of opening her mouth very wide when she talked, like a fish. You were perpetually seeing her tongue; and, what made it worse, her tongue was generally white. Most distressing. And how the tongue wagged! In spite of its whiteness. Wagged like mad, and mostly about the Divine Mind.'

'The Divine Mind?'

He nodded. 'It was her speciality. In Rochester, N.Y., where she lived, she was never out of touch with it. You've no idea what a lot of Divine Mind there is floating about in Rochester, particularly in the neighbourhood of women with busy husbands and incomes of over fifteen thousand dollars. If only she could have stuck to the Divine Mind! But the Divine Mind has one grave defect: it won't make love to you. That was why she'd come all the way to Tunis in search of a merely human specimen.'

'And what did you do about it?'

'Stood it nine days and then took the boat to Sicily. Like a thief in the night. The wicked flee, you know. God, how they can flee!'

'And she?'

'Went back to Rochester, I suppose. But I never opened any more of her letters. Just dropped them into the fire whenever I saw the writing. Ostrichism – it's the only rational philosophy of conduct. According to the Freudians we're all unconsciously trying to get back to…'

'But poor woman!' Dodo burst out. 'She must have suffered.'

'Nothing like what I suffered. Besides, she had the Divine Mind to go back to; which was her version of the Freudians' pre-natal…'

'But I suppose you'd encouraged her to come to Tunis?'

Reluctantly, Fanning gave up his Freudians. 'She could write good letters,' he admitted. 'Inexplicably good, considering what she was at close range.'

'But then you treated her abominably.'

'But if you'd seen her, you'd realise how abominably she'd treated me.'

'You?'

'Yes, abominably – by merely existing. She taught me to be very shy of letters. That was why I was so pleasantly surprised this morning when my latest correspondent suddenly materialised at Cook's. Really ravishing. One could forgive her everything for the sake of her face and that charming body. Everything, even the vamping. For a vamp I suppose she is, even this one. That is, if a woman *can* be a spiritual adventuress when she's so young and pretty and well made. Absolutely and *sub specie aeternitatis*,[4] I suppose she can. But from the sublunary point of view of the male victim, I doubt whether, at twenty-one…'

'Only twenty-one?' Dodo was disapproving. 'But Miles!'

Fanning ignored her interruption. 'And another thing you must remember,' he went on, 'is that the spiritual vamp who's come of age this year is not at all the same as the spiritual vamp who came of age fifteen, twenty, twenty-five years ago. She doesn't bother much about Mysticism, or the Lower Classes, or the Divine Mind, or any nonsense of that sort. No, she goes straight to the real point – the point which the older vamps approached in such a tiresomely circuitous fashion – she goes straight to herself. But straight!'

He stabbed the air with his fruit-knife.

'A bee-line. Oh, it has a certain charm, that directness. But whether it won't be rather frightful when they're older is another question. But then almost everything is rather frightful when people are older.'

'Thank you,' said Dodo. 'And what about you?'

'Oh, an old satyr,' he answered with that quick, brilliantly mysterious smile of his. 'A superannuated faun. I know it; only too well. But at the same time, most intolerably, a Higher Person. Which is what draws the spiritual vamps. Even the youngest ones. Not to talk to me about the Divine Mind, of course, or their views about Social Reform. But about themselves. Their Individualities, their Souls, their Inhibitions, their Unconsciouses, their Pasts, their Futures. For them, the Higher Things are all frankly and nakedly personal. And the function of the Higher Person is to act as a sort of psychoanalytical father confessor. He exists to tell them all about their strange and wonderful psyches. And meanwhile, of course, his friendship inflates their egotism. And if there should be any question of love, what a personal triumph!'

'Which is all very well,' objected Dodo. 'But what about the old satyr? Wouldn't it also be a bit of a triumph for him? You know, Miles,' she added gravely, 'it would really be scandalous if you were to take advantage...'

'But I haven't the slightest intention of taking any advantages. If only for my own sake. Besides, the child is too ingenuously absurd. The most hair-raising theoretical knowledge of life, out of books. You should hear her prattle away about inverts and perverts and birth control – but prattling from unplumbed depths of innocence and practical ignorance. Very queer. And touching too. Much more touching than the old-fashioned innocences of the young creatures who thought babies were brought by storks. Knowing all about love and lust, but in the same way as one knows all about quadratic equations. And her knowledge of the other aspects of life is really of the same kind. What she's seen of the world she's seen in her mother's company. The worst guide imaginable, to judge from the child's account. (Dead now, incidentally.) The sort of woman who could never live on top gear, so to speak – only at one or two imaginative removes from the facts. So that, in her company, what was nominally real life became actually just literature – yet more literature. Bad, inadequate Balzac in flesh and blood instead of genuine, good Balzac out of a set of nice green volumes. The child realises it herself. Obscurely, of course; but distressfully. It's one of the reasons why she's applied to me; she hopes I can explain what's wrong. And correct it in practice. Which I won't do in any drastic manner, I promise you. Only mildly, by precept – that is, if I'm not too bored to do it at all.'

'What's the child's name?' Dodo asked.

'Pamela Tarn.'

'Tarn? But was her mother by any chance Clare Tarn?'

He nodded. 'That was it. She even made her daughter call her by her Christian name. The companion stunt.'

'But I used to know Clare Tarn quite well,' said Dodo in an astonished, feeling voice. 'These last years I've hardly seen her. But when I was more in London just after the War…'

'But this begins to be interesting,' said Fanning. 'New light on my little friend…'

'Whom I absolutely forbid you,' said Dodo emphatically, 'to…'

'Tamper with the honour of,' he suggested. 'Let's phrase it as nobly as possible.'

'No, seriously, Miles. I really won't have it. Poor Clare Tarn's daughter. If I didn't have to rush off tomorrow I'd ask her to come and see me, so as to warn her.'

Fanning laughed. 'She wouldn't thank you. And besides, if anyone is to be warned, I'm the one who's in danger. But I shall be firm, Dodo – a rock. I won't allow her to seduce me.'

'You're incorrigible, Miles. But mind, if you dare…'

'But I won't. Definitely.' His tone was reassuring. 'Meanwhile I must hear something about the mother.'

The marchesa shrugged her shoulders. 'A woman who couldn't live on top gear. You've really said the last word.'

'But I want first words,' he answered. 'It's not the verdict that's interesting. It's the whole case, it's all the evidence. You're subpoenaed, my dear. Speak up.'

'Poor Clare!'

'Oh, *nil nisi bonum*,[5] of course, if that's what disturbs you.'

'She'd have so loved it to be not *bonum*, poor dear!' said the marchesa, tempering her look of vague condolence with a little smile. 'That was her great ambition – to be thought rather wicked. She'd have liked to have the reputation of a vampire. Not a spiritual one, mind you. The other sort. Lola Montes – that was her ideal.'

'It's an ideal,' said Fanning, 'that takes some realising, I can tell you.'

Dodo nodded. 'And that's what she must have found out, pretty soon. She wasn't born to be a fatal woman; she lacked the gifts. No staggering beauty, no mysterious fascination or intoxicating vitality. She was just very charming, that was all; and at the same time rather impossible and absurd. So that there weren't any aspiring victims to be fatal to. And a vampire without victims is – well *what*?'

'Certainly not a vampire,' he concluded.

'Except, of course, in her own imagination, if she chooses to think so. In her own imagination Clare certainly was a vampire.'

'Reduced, in fact, to being her own favourite character in fiction.'

'Precisely. You always find the phrase.'

'Only too fatally!' He made a little grimace. 'I often wish I didn't. The luxury of being inarticulate! To be able to wallow indefinitely long in every feeling and sensation, instead of having to clamber out at once on to a hard, dry, definite phrase. But what about your Clare?'

'Well, she started, of course, by being a riddle to me. Unanswerable, or rather answerable, answered, but so very strangely that I was still left wondering. I shall never forget the first time Filippo and I went to dine there. Poor Roger Tarn was still alive then. While the men were drinking their port, Clare and I were alone in the drawing room. There was a little chit-chat, I remember, and then, with a kind of determined despera-tion, as though she'd that second screwed herself up to jumping off the Eiffel Tower, suddenly, out of the blue, she asked me if I'd ever had one of those *wonderful* Sicilian peasants – I can't possibly reproduce the tone, the expression – as a lover. I was a bit taken aback, I must confess. "But we don't live in Sicily," was the only thing I could think of answering – too idiotically! "Our estates are all in Umbria and Tuscany." "But the Tuscans are *superb* creatures too," she insisted. Superb, I agreed. But, as it happens, I don't have affairs with even the superbest peasants. Nor with anybody else, for that matter. Clare was dreadfully disappointed. I think she'd expected the most romantic confid-ences – moonlight and mandolines and *stretti, stretti, nell'estasi d'amor*.[6] She was really very ingenuous. "Do you mean to say you've really never…?" she insisted. I ought to have got angry, I suppose; but it was all so ridiculous, that I never thought of it. I just said, "Never," and felt as though I were refusing her a favour. But she made up for my churlishness by being lavish to herself. But lavish! You can't imagine what a tirade she let fly at me. How *wonderful* it was to get away from self-conscious, complicated, sentimental love! How profoundly *satisfying* to feel oneself at the mercy of the dumb, dark forces of physical passion! How *intoxicating* to humiliate one's culture and one's class feeling before some *magnificent* primitive, some *earthily* beautiful satyr, some *divine* animal! And so on, *crescendo*. And it ended with her telling me the story of her *extraordinary* affair with – was it a gamekeeper? or a young farmer? I forget. But there was something about rabbit-shooting in it, I know.'

'It sounds like a chapter out of George Sand.'

'It was.'

'Or still more, I'm afraid,' he said, making a wry face, 'like a most deplorable parody of my *Endymion and the Moon*.'

'Which I've never read, I'm ashamed to say.'

'You should, if only to understand this Clare of yours.'

'I will. Perhaps I'd have solved her more quickly, if I'd read it at the time. As it was I could only be amazed – and a little horrified. That rabbit-shooter!' She shook her head. 'He ought to have been so romantic. But I could only think of that awful yellow kitchen soap he'd be sure to wash himself with, or perhaps carbolic, so that he'd smell like washed dogs – dreadful! And the flannel shirts, not changed quite often enough. And the hands, so horny, with very short nails, perhaps broken. No, I simply couldn't understand her.'

'Which is to your discredit, Dodo, if I may say so.'

'Perhaps. But you must admit, I never pretended to be anything but what I am – a perfectly frivolous and respectable member of the upper classes. With a taste, I must confess, for the scandalous. Which was one of the reasons, I suppose, why I became so intimate with poor Clare. I was really fascinated by her confidences.'

'Going on the tiles vicariously, eh?'

'Well, if you choose to put it grossly and vulgarly...'

'Which I *do* choose,' he interposed. 'To be tactfully gross and appositely vulgar – that, my dear, is one of the ultimate artistic refinements. One day I shall write a monograph on the aesthetics of vulgarity. But meanwhile shall we say that you were inspired by an intense scientific curiosity to…'

Dodo laughed. 'One of the tiresome things about you, Miles, is that one can never go on being angry with you.'

'Yet another subject for a monograph!' he answered, and his smile was at once confidential and ironical, affectionate and full of mockery. 'But let's hear what the scientific curiosity elicited?'

'Well, to begin with, a lot of really rather embarrassingly intimate confidences and questions, which I needn't repeat.'

'No, don't. I know what those feminine conversations are. I have a native modesty…'

'Oh, so have I. And, strangely enough, so had Clare. But somehow she wanted to outrage herself. You felt it all the time. She always had that desperate jumping-off-the-Eiffel-Tower manner, when she began to talk like that. It was a kind of martyrdom. But enjoyable. Perversely.'

Dodo shook her head.

'Very puzzling. I used to have to make quite an effort to change the conversation from gynaecology to romance. Oh, those lovers of hers! Such stories! The most fantastic adventures in East End opium dens, in aeroplanes, and even, I remember (it was that very hot summer of 'twenty-two), even in a refrigerator!'

'My dear!' protested Fanning.

'Honestly! I'm only repeating what she told me.'

'But do you mean to say you believed her?'

'Well, by that time, I must admit, I was beginning to be rather sceptical. You see, I could never elicit the names of these creatures. Nor any detail. It was as though they didn't exist outside the refrigerator and the aeroplane.'

'How many of them were there?'

'Only two at that particular moment. One was a Grand Passion, and the other a Caprice. A Caprice,' she repeated, rolling the r. 'It was one of poor Clare's favourite words. I used to try and pump her. But she was mum. "I want them to be *mysterious*," she told me the last time I pressed her for details, "anonymous, without an *état civil*. Why should I show you their pass-ports and identity cards?" "Perhaps they haven't got any," I suggested. Which was malicious. I could see she was annoyed. But a week later she showed me their photographs. There they were; the camera cannot lie; I had to be convinced. The Grand Passion, I must say, was a very striking-looking creature. Thin-faced, worn, a bit Roman and sinister. The Caprice was more ordinarily the nice young Englishman. Rather childish and simple, Clare explained; and she gave me to understand that she was initiating him. It was the other, the Grand P., who thought of such refinements as the refrigerator. Also, she now confided to me for the first time, he was mildly a sadist. Having seen his face, I could believe it. "Am I ever likely to meet him?" I asked. She shook her head. He moved in a very different world from mine.'

'A rabbit-shooter?' Fanning asked.

'No: an intellectual. That's what I gathered.'

'Golly!'

'So there was not the slightest probability, as you can see, that *I* should ever meet him,' Dodo laughed. 'And yet almost the first face I saw on leaving Clare that afternoon was the Grand P.'s.'

'Coming to pay his sadistic respects?'

'Alas for poor Clare, no. He was behind glass in the show-case of a photographer in the Brompton Road, not a hundred yards from the Tarns' house in Ovington Square. The identical portrait. I marched straight in. "Can you tell me who that is?" But it appears that photography is done under the seal of confession. They wouldn't say. Could I order a copy? Well, yes, as a favour, they'd let me have one. Curiously enough, they told me, as they were taking down my name and address, another lady had come in only two or three days before and also ordered a copy. "Not by any chance a rather tall lady with light auburn hair and a rather amusing mole on the left cheek?" That did rather sound like the lady. "And with a very confidential manner," I suggested, "as though you were her oldest friends?" Exactly, exactly; they were unanimous. That clinched it. Poor Clare, I thought, as I walked on towards the park, poor, poor Clare!'

There was a silence.

'Which only shows,' said Fanning at last, 'how right the Church has always been to persecute literature. The harm we imaginative writers do! Enormous! We ought all to be on the Index, every one. Consider your Clare, for example. If it hadn't been for books, she'd never have known that such things as passion and sensuality and perversity even existed. Never.'

'Come, come,' she protested.

But, 'Never,' Fanning repeated. 'She was congenitally as cold as a fish; it's obvious. Never had a spontaneous, untutored desire in her life. But she'd read a lot of books. Out of which she'd fabricated a theory of passion and perversity. Which she then consciously put into practice.'

'Or rather didn't put into practice. Only daydreamed that she did.'

He nodded. 'For the most part. But sometimes, I don't mind betting, she realised the daydreams in actual life. Desperately, as you so well described it, with her teeth clenched and her eyes shut, as though she were jumping off the Eiffel Tower. That rabbit-shooter, for instance...'

'But do you think the rabbit-shooter really existed?'

'Perhaps not that particular one. But *a* rabbit-shooter, perhaps several rabbit-shooters – at one time or another, I'm sure, they genuinely existed. Though never *genuinely*, of course, for her. For her, it's obvious, they were just phantoms, like the other inhabitants of her dreamery. Phantoms of flesh and blood, but still phantoms. I see her as a kind of Midas, turning everything she touched into imagination. Even in the embraces of a genuine, solid rabbit-shooter, she was still only indulging in her solitary sultry dream – a dream inspired by Shakespeare, or Mrs Barclay, or the Chevalier de Nerciat, or D'Annunzio, or whoever her favourite author may have been.'

'Miles Fanning, perhaps,' Dodo mockingly suggested.

'Yes, I feared as much.'

'What a responsibility!'

'Which I absolutely refuse to accept. What have I ever written but solemn warnings against the vice of imagination? Sermons against mental licentiousness of every kind – intellectual licentiousness, mystical licentiousness, fantastic-amorous licentiousness. No, no. I'll accept no responsibility. Or at least no special responsibility – only the generic responsibility of being an imaginative author, the original sin of writing in such a way as to influence people. And when I say "influence", of course I don't really mean *influence*. Because a writer can't influence people, in the sense of making them think and feel and act as he does. He can only influence them to be more, or less, like one of their own selves. In other words, he's never understood. (Thank goodness! because it would be very humiliating to be really understood by one's readers.) What readers get out of him is never, finally, *his* ideas, but theirs. And when they try to imitate him or his creations, all that they can ever do is to act one of their own potential *rôles*. Take this particular case. Clare read and, I take it, was impressed. She took my warnings against mental licentiousness to heart and proceeded to do – what? Not to become a creature of spontaneous, unvitiated impulses – for the good reason that that wasn't in her power – but only to imagine that she was such a creature. She imagined herself a woman like the one I put into *Endymion and the*

Moon and acted accordingly – or else didn't act, only dreamed; it makes very little difference. In a word, she did exactly what all my books told her not to do. Inevitably; it was her nature. I'd influenced her, yes. But she didn't become more like one of my heroines. She only became more intensely like herself. And then, you must remember, mine weren't the only books on her shelves. I think we can take it that she'd read *Les Liaisons Dangereuses* and Casanova and some biography, shall we say, of the Maréchal de Richelieu. So that those spontaneous unvitiated impulses – how ludicrous they are, anyhow, when you *talk* about them! – became identified in her mind with the most elegant forms of "caprice" – wasn't that the word? She was a child of nature – but with qualifications. The kind of child of nature that lived at Versailles or on the Grand Canal about 1760. Hence those rabbit-shooters and hence also those sadistic intellectuals, whether real or imaginary – and imaginary even when real. I may have been a favourite author. But I'm not responsible for the rabbit-shooter or the Grand Ps. Not more responsible than anyone else. She'd heard of the existence of love before she'd read me. We're all equally to blame, from Homer downwards, Plato wouldn't have any of us in his Republic. He was quite right, I believe. Quite right.'

'And what about the daughter?' Dodo asked, after a silence.

He shrugged his shoulders. 'In reaction against the mother, so far as I could judge. In reaction, but also influenced by her, unconsciously. And the influence is effective because, after all, she's her mother's daughter and probably resembles her mother, congenitally. But consciously, on the surface, she knows she doesn't want to live as though she were in a novel. And yet can't help it, because that's her nature, that's how she was brought up. But she's miserable, because she realises that fiction-life *is* fiction. Miserable and very anxious to get out – out through the covers of the novel into the real world.'

'And are you her idea of the real world?' Dodo enquired.

He laughed, 'Yes, I'm the real world. Strange as it may seem. And also, of course, pure fiction. The Writer, the Great Man – the Official Biographer's fiction, in a word. Or, better still, the autobiographer's fiction. Chateaubriand, shall we say. And her breaking out – that's fiction too. A pure Miles Fanningism, if ever there was one. And, poor child, she knows it. Which makes her so cross with herself. Cross with me too, in a curious obscure way. But at the same time she's thrilled. What a thrilling situation! And herself walking about in the middle of it. She looks on and wonders and wonders what the next instalment of the feuilleton's going to contain.'

'Well, there's one thing we're quite certain it's not going to contain, aren't we? Remember your promise, Miles.'

'I think of nothing else,' he bantered.

'Seriously, Miles, seriously.'

'I think of nothing else,' he repeated in a voice that was the parody of a Shakespearean actor's.

Dodo shook her finger at him. 'Mind,' she said, 'mind!' Then, pushing back her chair, 'Let's move into the drawing room,' she went on. 'We shall be more comfortable there.'

4

'And to think,' Pamela was writing in her diary, 'how nervous I'd been beforehand, and the trouble I'd taken to work out the whole of our first meeting, question and answer, like the Shorter Catechism, instead of which I was like a fish in water, really at home, for the first time in my life, I believe. No, perhaps not more at home than with Ruth and Phyllis, but then they're girls, so they hardly count. Besides, when you've once been at home in the sea, it doesn't seem much fun being at home in a little glass bowl, which is rather unfair to Ruth and Phyllis, but after all it's not their fault and they can't help being little bowls, just as M.F. can't help being a sea, and when you've swum about a bit in all that intelligence and knowledge and really *devilish* understanding, well, you find the bowls rather narrow, though of course they're sweet little bowls and I shall always be very fond of them, especially Ruth. Which makes me wonder if what he said about Clare and me – unnatural by nature – is always true, because hasn't every unnatural person got somebody she can be natural with, or even that she can't help being natural with, like oxygen and that other stuff making water? Of course it's not guaranteed that you find the other person who makes you natural, and I think perhaps Clare never did find her person, because I don't believe it was Daddy. But in any case there's Ruth and Phyllis and now today M.F.; and he really proves it, because I *was* natural with him more than with anyone, even though he did say I was unnatural by nature. No, I feel that if I were with him always, I should always be my *real* self, just kind of easily spouting, like those lovely fountains we went to look at this afternoon, not all tied up in knots and squirting about vaguely in every kind of direction, and muddy at that, but beautifully clear in a big gushing spout, like what Joan in *The Return of Eurydice* finally became when she'd

49

escaped from that awful, awful man and found Walter. But does that mean I'm in love with him?'

Pamela bit the end of her pen and stared, frowning, at the page before her. Scrawled large in orange ink, the question stared back. Disquietingly and insistently stared. She remembered a phrase of her mother's. 'But if you knew,' Clare had cried (Pamela could *see* her, wearing the black afternoon dress from Patou, and there were yellow roses in the bowl on the table under the window), 'if you knew what certain writers were to me! *Shrines* – there's no other word. I could worship the Tolstoy of *Anna Karenina*.' But Harry Braddon, to whom the words were addressed, had laughed at her. And, though she hated Harry Braddon, so had Pamela, mockingly. For it was absurd; nobody was a shrine, nobody. And anyway, what *was* a shrine? Nothing. Not nowadays, not when one had stopped being a child. She told herself these things with a rather unnecessary emphasis, almost truculently, in the style of the professional atheists in Hyde Park. One didn't worship – for the good reason that she herself once had worshipped. Miss Figgis, the classical mistress, had been her pash for more than a year. Which was why she had gone to early service so frequently in those days and been so keen to go up to Oxford and take Greats. (Besides, she had even, at that time, rather liked and admired Miss Huss. Ghastly old Hussy! It seemed incredible now.) But oh, that grammar! And Caesar was such a bore, and Livy still worse, and as for Greek... She had tried very hard for a time. But when Miss Figgis so obviously preferred that priggish little beast Kathleen, Pamela had just let things slide. The bad marks had come in torrents and old Hussy had begun being more sorrowful than angry, and finally more angry than sorrowful. But she hadn't cared. What made not caring easier was that she had her mother behind her. 'I'm so delighted,' was what Clare had said when she heard that Pamela had given up wanting to go to Oxford. 'I'd have felt so terribly inferior if you'd turned out a blue-stocking. Having my frivolity rebuked by my own daughter!'

Clare had always boasted of her frivolity. Once, under the influence of old Hussy and for the love of Miss Figgis, an earnest disapprover, Pamela had become an apostle of her mother's gospel. 'After all,' she had pointed out to Miss Figgis, 'Cleopatra didn't learn Greek.' And though Miss Figgis was able to point out, snubbingly, that the last of the Ptolemies had probably spoken nothing but Greek, Pamela could still insist that in principle she was quite right: Cleopatra hadn't learnt Greek, or what, if you were Greek, corresponded to Greek. So why should she? She began to parade a violent and childish cynicism, a cynicism which was still (though she had learnt, since leaving school, to temper the ridiculous expression of it) her official creed. There were no shrines – though she some-times, wistfully and rather shamefacedly, wished there were. One didn't, determinedly didn't worship. She herself might admire Fanning's books, *did* admire them, enormously. But as for worshipping – no, she absolutely declined. Clare had over-done it all somehow – as usual. Pamela was resolved that there should be no nonsense about *her* feelings.

'But does that mean I'm in love with him?' insisted the orange scrawl. As though in search of an answer, Pamela turned back the pages of her diary (she had already covered nearly eight of them with her account of this memorable twelfth of June).

'His face,' she read, 'is very brown, almost like an Arab's, except that he has blue eyes, as he lives mostly in the South, because he says that if you don't live in the sun, you go slightly mad, which is why people in the North, like us and the Germans and the Americans, are so tiresome, though of course you go still madder where there's too much sun, like in India, where they're even more hopeless. He's very good-looking and you don't think of him as being either old or young, but just as being there, like that, and the way he smiles is really very extraordinary, and so are his eyes, and I simply *adored* his white silk suit.'

But the question was not yet answered. His silk suit wasn't him, nor was his voice, even though he had 'an awfully nice one, rather like that man who talks about books on the wireless, only nicer'. She turned over a page. 'But M.F. is different from most clever people,' the orange scrawl proclaimed, 'because he doesn't make you feel a fool, even when he does laugh at you, and never, which is so *ghastly* with men like Professor Cobley, talks down to you in that awful patient, gentle way, which makes you feel a million times more of a worm than being snubbed or ignored, because, if you have any pride, that sort of intelligence without tears is just loathsome, as though you were being given a milk pudding out of charity. No, M.F. talks to you on the level, and the extraordinary thing is that, while he's talking to you and you're talking to him, you *are* on a level with him, or at any rate you feel as though you were, which comes to the same thing. He's like influenza, you catch his intelligence.'

Pamela let the leaves of the notebook flick past, one by one, under her thumb. The final words on the half-blank page once more stared at her, questioningly. 'But does that mean I'm in love with him?' Taking her pen from between her teeth, 'Certainly,' she wrote, 'I do find him terribly attractive physically.' She paused for a moment to reflect, then added, frowning as though with the effort of raising an elusive fact from the depths of memory, of solving a difficult problem in algebra, 'Because really, when he put his hand on my shoulder, which would have been simply intolerable if anyone else had done it, but somehow with him I didn't mind, I felt all thrilled with an absolute *frisson*.' She ran her pen through the last word and substituted 'thrill', which she underlined to make it seem less lamely a repetition. '*Frisson*' had been one of Clare's favourite words; hearing it pronounced in her mother's remembered voice, Pamela had felt a sudden mistrust of it; it seemed to cast a kind of doubt on the feelings it stood for, a doubt of which she was ashamed – it seemed so disloyal and the voice had sounded so startlingly, so heart-rendingly clear and near – but which she still couldn't help experiencing. She defended herself; '*frisson*' had simply to go, because the thrill was genuine, absolutely genuine, she insisted.

'For a moment,' she went on, writing very fast, as though she were trying to run away from the sad, disagreeable thoughts that had intruded upon her, 'I thought I was going to faint when he touched me, like when one's coming to after chloroform, which I've certainly never felt like with anyone else.' As a protest against the doubts inspired by that unfortunate frisson she underlined 'never', heavily. Never; it was quite true. When Harry Braddon had tried to kiss her, she had been furious and disgusted – disgusting beast! Saddening and reproachful, Clare's presence hovered round her once more; Clare had liked Harry Braddon. Still, he was a beast. Pamela had never told her mother about that kiss.

She shut her eyes excludingly and thought instead of Cecil Rudge, poor, timid, unhappy little Cecil, whom she liked so much, was so genuinely sorry for. But when, that afternoon at Aunt Edith's, when at last, after an hour's visibly laborious screwing to the sticking point, he had had the courage to take her hand and say 'Pamela' and kiss it, she had just laughed, oh! unforgivably, but she simply couldn't help it; he was so ridiculous. Poor lamb, he had been terribly upset. 'But I'm so sorry,' she had gasped between the bursts of her laughter, 'so dreadfully sorry. Please don't be hurt.' But his face, she could see, was agonised. 'Please! Oh, I feel so miserable.' And she had gone off into another explosion of laughter which almost choked her. But when she could breathe again, she had run to him where he stood, averted and utterly unhappy, by the window, she had taken his hand and, when he still refused to look at her, had put her arm round his neck and kissed him. But the emotion that had filled her eyes with tears was nothing like passion.

As for Hugh Davies – why, it certainly had been rather thrilling when Hugh kissed her. It had been thrilling, but certainly not to fainting point. But then had she *really* felt like fainting today? a small voice questioned. She drowned the small voice with the scratching of her pen. 'Consult the oracles of passion,' she wrote and, laying down her pen, got up and crossed the room. A copy of *The Return of Eurydice* was lying on the bed; she picked it up and turned over the pages. Here it was!

'Consult the oracles of passion,' she read aloud, and her own voice sounded, she thought, strangely oracular in the solitude. 'A god speaks in them, or else a devil, one can never tell which beforehand, nor even, in most cases, afterwards. And, when all is said, does it very much matter? God and devil are equally supernatural, that is the important thing; equally supernatural and therefore, in this all too flatly natural world of sense and science and society, equally desirable, equally significant.'

She shut the book and walked back to the table. 'Which is what he said this afternoon,' she went on writing, 'but in that laughing way, when I said I could never see why one shouldn't do what one liked, instead of all this Hussy and Hippo rigmarole about service and duty, and he said yes, that was what Rabelais had said' (there seemed to be an awful lot of 'saids' in this sentence, but it couldn't be helped; she scrawled on); 'which I pretended I'd read – why can't one tell the truth? particularly as I'd just been saying at the same time that one ought to say what one thinks as well as do what one likes; but it seems to be hopeless – and he said he entirely agreed, it was perfect, so long as you had the luck to like the sort of things that kept you on the right side of the prison bars and think the sort of things that don't get you murdered when you say them. And I said I'd rather say what I thought and do what I liked and be murdered and put in gaol than be a Hippo, and he said I was an idealist, which annoyed me and I said I certainly wasn't, all I was was someone who didn't want to go mad with inhibitions. And he laughed, and I wanted to quote him his own words about the oracles, but somehow it was so shy-making that I didn't. All the same, it's what I intensely feel, that one *ought* to consult the oracles of passion. And I shall consult them.'

She leaned back in her chair and shut her eyes. The orange question floated across the darkness, 'But does that mean I'm in love with him?' The oracle seemed to be saying yes. But oracles, she resolutely refused to remember, can be rigged to suit the interests of the questioner. Didn't the admirer of *The Return of Eurydice* secretly *want* the oracle to say yes? Didn't she think she'd almost fainted, because she'd wished she'd almost fainted, because she'd come desiring to faint? Pamela sighed; then, with a gesture of decision, she slapped her notebook to and put away her pen. It was time to get ready for dinner; she bustled about efficiently and distractingly among her trunks. But the question returned to her as she lay soaking in the warm otherworld of her bath. By the time she got out she had boiled herself to such a pitch of giddiness that she could hardly stand.

For Pamela, dinner in solitude, especially the public solitude of hotels, was a punishment. Companionlessness and compulsory silence depressed her. Besides, she never felt quite eye-proof; she could never escape from the obsession that everyone was looking at her, judging, criticising. Under a carapace of rather impertinent uncaringness she writhed distressfully. At Florence her loneliness had driven her to make friends with two not very young American women who were staying in her hotel. They were a bit earnest and good and dreary. But Pamela preferred even dreariness to solitude. She attached herself to them inseparably. They were touched. When she left for Rome, they promised to write to her, they made her promise to write to them. She was so young; they felt responsible; a steadying hand, the counsel of older friends… Pamela had already received two steadying letters. But she hadn't answered them, never would answer them. The horrors of lonely dining cannot be alleviated by correspondence.

Walking down to her ordeal in the restaurant, she positively yearned for her dreary friends. But the hall was a desert of alien eyes and faces; and the waiter who led her through the hostile dining room had bowed, it seemed to her, with ironical politeness, and mockingly smiled. She sat down haughtily at her table and almost wished she were under it. When the sommelier appeared with his list, she ordered half a bottle of something absurdly expensive, for fear he might think she didn't know anything about wine.

She had got as far as the fruit, when a presence loomed over her; she looked up. 'You?' Her delight was an illumination; the young man was dazzled. 'What a marvellous luck!' Yet it was only Guy Browne, Guy whom she had met a few times at dances and found quite pleasant – that was all. 'Think of your being in Rome!' She made him sit down at her table. When she had finished her coffee, Guy suggested that they should go out and dance somewhere. They went. It was nearly three when Pamela got to bed. She had had a most enjoyable evening.

5

But how ungratefully she treated poor Guy when, next day at lunch, Fanning asked her how she had spent the evening! True, there were extenuating circumstances, chief among which was the fact that Fanning had kissed her when they met. By force of habit, he himself would have explained, if anyone had asked him why, because he kissed every presentable face. Kissing was in the great English tradition. 'It's the only way I can be like Chaucer,' he liked to affirm. 'Just as knowing a little Latin and less Greek is my only claim to resembling Shakespeare and as lying bed till ten's the nearest I get to Descartes.'

In this particular case, as perhaps in every other particular case, the force of habit had been seconded by a deliberate intention; he was accustomed to women being rather in love with him, he liked the amorous atmosphere and could use the simplest as well as the most complicated methods to create it. Moreover he was an experimentalist, he genuinely wanted to see what would happen. What happened was that Pamela was astonished, embarrassed, thrilled, delighted, bewildered. And what with her confused excitement and the enormous effort she had made to take it all as naturally and easily as he had done, she was betrayed into what, in other circumstances, would have been a scandalous ingratitude. But when one has just been kissed, for the first time and at one's second meeting with him, kissed offhandedly and yet (she felt it) significantly, by Miles Fanning – actually Miles Fanning! – little men like Guy Browne do seem rather negligible, even though one did have a very good time with them the evening before.

'I'm afraid you must have been rather lonely last night,' said Fanning, as they sat down to lunch. His sympathy hypocritically covered a certain satisfaction that it should be his absence that had condemned her to dreariness.

'No, I met a friend,' Pamela answered with a smile which the inward comparison of Guy with the author of *The Return of Eurydice* had tinged with a certain amused condescendingness.

'A friend?' He raised his eyebrows. '*Amico* or *amica*? Our English is so discreetly equivocal. With this key Bowdler locked up his heart. But I apologise. *Co* or *ca*?'

'*Co*. He's called Guy Browne and he's here learning Italian to get into the Foreign Office. He's a nice boy.' Pamela might have been talking about a favourite, or even not quite favourite, retriever. 'Nice; but nothing very special. I mean, not in the way of intelligence.'

She shook her head patronisingly over Guy's very creditable First in History as a guttersnipe capriciously favoured by an archduke might learn in his protector's company to shake his head and patronisingly smile at the name of a marquis of only four or five centuries' standing.

'He can dance, though,' she admitted.

'So I suppose you danced with him?' said Fanning in a tone which, in spite of his amusement at the child's assumption of an aged superiority, he couldn't help making rather disobligingly sarcastic. It annoyed him to think that Pamela should have spent an evening, which he had pictured as dismally lonely, dancing with a young man.

'Yes, we danced,' said Pamela, nodding.

'Where?'

'Don't ask me. We went to about six different places in the course of the evening.'

'Of course you did,' said Fanning almost bitterly. 'Moving rapidly from one place to another and doing exactly the same thing in each – that seems to be the young's ideal of bliss.'

Speaking as a young who had risen above such things, but who still had to suffer from the folly of her unregenerate contemporaries, 'It's quite true,' Pamela gravely confirmed.

'They go to Pekin to listen to the wireless and to Benares to dance the foxtrot. I've seen them at it. It's incomprehensible. And then the tooting up and down in automobiles, and the roaring up and down in aeroplanes, and the stinking up and down in motor boats. Up and down, up and down, just for the sake of not sitting still, of having never time to think or feel. No, I give them up, these young of yours.' He shook his head. 'But I'm becoming a minor prophet,' he added; his good humour was beginning to return.

'But after all,' said Pamela, 'we're not *all* like that.'

Her gravity made him laugh. 'There's at least one who's ready to let herself be bored by a tiresome survivor from another civilistion. Thank you, Pamela.' Leaning across the table, he took her hand and kissed it. 'I've been horribly ungrateful,' he went on, and his face as he looked at her was suddenly transfigured by the bright enigmatic beauty of his smile. 'If you knew how charming you looked!' he said; and it was true. The ingenuous face, those impertinent little breasts – charming. 'And how charming you *were*! But of course you *do* know,' a little demon prompted him to add, 'no doubt Mr Browne told you last night.'

Pamela had blushed – a blush of pleasure, and embarrassed shyness, and excitement. What he had just said and done was more significant, she felt, even than the kiss he had given her when they met. Her cheeks burned; but she managed, with an effort, to keep her eyes unwaveringly on his. His last words made her frown.

'He certainly didn't,' she answered. 'He'd have got his face smacked.'

'Is that a delicate hint?' he asked. 'If so,' and he leaned forward, 'here's the other cheek.'

Her face went redder than ever. She felt suddenly miserable; he was only laughing at her. 'Why do you laugh at me?' she said aloud, unhappily.

'But I wasn't,' he protested. 'I really did think you were annoyed.'

'But why should I have been?'

'I can't imagine.' He smiled. 'But if you would have smacked Mr Browne's face...'

'But Guy's quite different.'

It was Fanning's turn to wince. 'You mean he's young, while I'm only a poor old imbecile who needn't be taken seriously?'

'Why are you so stupid?' Pamela asked almost fiercely. 'No, but I mean,' she added in quick apology, 'I mean... well, I don't care two pins about Guy. So you see, it would annoy me if he tried to push in, like that. Whereas with somebody who does mean something to me...' Pamela hesitated. 'With *you*,' she specified in a rather harsh, strained voice and with just that look of despairing determination, Fanning imagined, just that jumping-off-the-Eiffel-Tower expression, which her mother's face must have assumed in moments such as this, 'it's quite different. I mean, with you of course I'm not annoyed. I'm pleased. Or at least I *was* pleased, till I saw you were just making a fool of me.'

Touched and flattered, 'But, my dear child,' Fanning protested, 'I wasn't doing anything of the kind. I meant what I said. And much more than I said,' he added, in the teeth of the warning and reproachful outcry raised by his common sense. It was amusing to experiment, it was pleasant to be adored, exciting to be tempted (and how young she was, how perversely fresh!). There was even something quite agreeable in resisting temptation; it had the charms of a strenuous and difficult sport. Like mountain climbing. He smiled once more, consciously brilliant.

This time Pamela dropped her eyes. There was a silence which might have protracted itself uncomfortably, if the waiter had not broken it by bringing the tagliatelle. They began to eat. Pamela was all at once exuberantly gay.

After coffee they took a taxi and drove to the Villa Giulia. 'For we mustn't,' Fanning explained, 'neglect your education.'

'Mustn't we?' she asked. 'I often wonder why we mustn't. Truthfully now, I mean without any hippoing and all that – why shouldn't I neglect it? Why should I go to this beastly museum?' She was preparing to play the cynical, boastfully unintellectual part which she had made her own. 'Why?' she repeated truculently. Behind the rather vulgar lowbrow mask she cultivated wistful yearnings and concealed the uneasy consciousness of inferiority. 'A lot of beastly old Roman odds and ends!' she grumbled; that was one for Miss Figgis.

'Roman?' said Fanning. 'God forbid! Etruscan.'

'Well, Etruscan, then; it's all the same, anyhow. Why shouldn't I neglect the Etruscans? I mean, what have they got to do with me – *me*?' And she gave her chest two or three little taps with the tip of a crooked forefinger.

'Nothing, my child,' he answered. 'Thank goodness, they've absolutely nothing to do with you, or me, or anybody else.'

'Then why...?'

'Precisely for that reason. That's the definition of culture – knowing and thinking about things that have absolutely nothing to do with us. About Etruscans, for example; or the mountains on the moon; or cat's-cradle among the Chinese; or the universe at large.'

'All the same,' she insisted, 'I still don't see.'

'Because you've never known people who weren't cultured. But make the acquaintance of a few practical businessmen – the kind who have no time to be anything but alternately efficient and tired. Or of a few workmen from the big towns. (Country people are different; they still have the remains of the old substitutes for culture – religion, folklore, tradition. The town fellows have lost the substitutes without acquiring the genuine article.) Get to know those people; *they'll* make you see the point of culture. Just as the Sahara'll make you see the point of water. And for the same reason: they're arid.'

'That's all very well; but what about people like Professor Cobley?'

'Whom I've happily never met,' he said, 'but can reconstruct from the expression on your face. Well, all that can be said about those people is: just try to imagine them if they'd never been irrigated. Gobi or Shamo.'

'Well, perhaps.' She was dubious.

'And anyhow the biggest testimony to culture isn't the soul-less philistines – it's the soulful ones. My sweet Pamela,' he implored, laying a hand on her bare brown arm, 'for heaven's sake don't run the risk of becoming a soulful philistine.'

'But as I don't know what that is,' she answered, trying to persuade herself, as she spoke, that the touch of his hand was giving her a tremendous *frisson* – but it really wasn't.

'It's what the name implies,' he said. 'A person without culture who goes in for having a soul. An illiterate idealist. A Higher Thinker with nothing to think about but his – or more often, I'm afraid, *her* – beastly little personal feelings and sensations. They spend their lives staring at their own navels and in the intervals trying to find other people who'll take an interest and come and stare too. Oh, figuratively,' he added, noticing the expression of astonishment which had passed across her face. '*En tout bien, tout honneur*.[7] At least, sometimes and to begin with. Though I've known cases...'

But he decided it would be better not to speak about the lady from Rochester, N.Y. Pamela might be made to feel that the cap fitted. Which it did, except that her little head was such a charming one.

'In the end,' he said, 'they go mad, these soulful philistines. Mad with self-consciousness and vanity and egotism and a kind of hopeless bewilderment; for when you're utterly without culture, every fact's an isolated, unconnected fact, every experience is unique and unprecedented. Your world's made up of a few bright points floating about inexplicably in the midst of an unfathomable darkness. Terrifying! It's enough to drive anyone mad. I've seen them, lots of them, gone utterly crazy. In the past they had organised religion, which meant that somebody had once been cultured for them, vicariously. But what with Protestantism and the modernists, their philistinism's absolute now. They're alone with their own souls. Which is the worst companionship a human being can have. So bad that it sends you dotty. So beware, Pamela, beware! You'll go mad if you think only of what has something to do with you. The Etruscans will keep you sane.'

'Let's hope so.' She laughed. 'But aren't we there?'

The cab drew up at the door of the villa; they got out.

'And remember that the things that start with having nothing to do with you,' said Fanning, as he counted out the money for the entrance tickets, 'turn out in the long run to have a great deal to do with you. Because they become a part of you and you of them. A soul can't know or fully become itself without knowing and therefore to some extent becoming what isn't itself. Which it does in various ways. By loving, for example.'

'You mean...?' The flame of interest brightened in her eyes.

But he went on remorselessly. 'And by thinking of things that have nothing to do with you.'

'Yes, I see.' The flame had dimmed again.

'Hence my concern about your education.' He beckoned her through the turnstile into the museum. 'A purely selfish concern,' he added, smiling down at her. 'Because I don't want the most charming of my young friends to grow into a monster, whom I shall be compelled to flee from. So resign yourself to the Etruscans.'

'I resign myself,' said Pamela, laughing. His words had made her feel happy and excited. 'You can begin.' And in a theatrical voice, like that which used to make Ruth go off into such fits of laughter, 'I am all ears,' she added, 'as they say in the Best Books.' She pulled off her hat and shook out the imprisoned hair.

To Fanning, as he watched her, the gesture brought a sudden shock of pleasure. The impatient, exuberant youthfulness of it! And the little head, so beautifully shaped, so gracefully and proudly poised on its long neck! And her hair was drawn back smoothly from the face to explode in a thick tangle of curls on the nape of the neck. Ravishing!

'All ears,' she repeated, delightfully conscious of the admiration she was receiving.

'All ears.' And almost meditatively, 'But do you know,' he went on, 'I've never even seen your ears. May I?' And without waiting for her permission, he lifted up the soft, goldy-brown hair that lay in a curve, drooping, along the side of her head.

Pamela's face violently reddened; but she managed nonetheless to laugh. 'Are they as long and furry as you expected?' she asked.

He allowed the lifted hair to fall back into its place and, without answering her question, 'I've always,' he said, looking at her with a smile which she found disquietingly enigmatic and remote, 'I've always had a certain fellow-feeling for those savages who collect ears and thread them on strings, as necklaces.'

'But what a horror!' she cried out.

'You think so?' He raised his eyebrows.

But perhaps, Pamela was thinking, he was a sadist. In that book of Krafft-Ebbing's there had been a lot about sadists. It would be queer if he were...

'But what's certain,' Fanning went on in another, business-like voice, 'what's only too certain is that ears aren't culture. They've got too much to do with us. With me, at any rate. Much too much.'

He smiled at her again. Pamela smiled back at him, fascinated and obscurely a little frightened; but the fright was an element in the fascination. She dropped her eyes.

'So don't let's waste any more time,' his voice went on. 'Culture to right of us, culture to left of us. Let's begin with this culture on the left. With the vases. They really have absolutely nothing to do with us.'

He began and Pamela listened. Not very attentively, however. She lifted her hand and, under the hair, touched her ear. 'A fellow-feeling for those savages.' She remembered his words with a little shudder. He'd almost meant them. And 'ears aren't culture. Too much to do with us. With me. Much too much.' He'd meant that too, genuinely and wholeheartedly. And his smile had been a confirmation of the words; yes, and a comment, full of mysterious significance. What *had* he meant? But surely it was obvious what he had meant. Or wasn't it obvious?

The face she turned towards him wore an expression of grave attention. And when he pointed to a vase and said, 'Look,' she looked, with what an air of concentrated intelligence! But as for knowing what he was talking about! She went on confusedly thinking that he had a fellow-feeling for those savages, and that her ears had too much to do with him, much too much, and that perhaps he was in love with her, perhaps also that he was like those people in Krafft-Ebbing, perhaps…; and it seemed to her that her blood must have turned into a kind of hot, red soda-water, all fizzy with little bubbles of fear and excitement.

She emerged, partially at least, out of this bubbly and agitated trance to hear him say, 'Look at that, now.' A tall statue towered over her. 'The Apollo of Veii,' he explained. 'And really, you know, it *is* the most beautiful statue in the world. Each time I see it, I'm more firmly convinced of that.'

Dutifully, Pamela stared. The god stood there on his pedestal, one foot advanced, erect in his draperies. He had lost his arms, but the head was intact and the strange Etruscan face was smiling, enigmatically smiling. Rather like *him*, it suddenly occurred to her.

'What's it made of?' she asked; for it was time to be intelligent.

'Terracotta. Originally coloured.'

'And what date?'

'Late sixth century.'

'BC?' she queried, a little dubiously, and was relieved when he nodded. It really would have been rather awful if it had been AD. 'Who by?'

'By Vulca, they say. But as that's the only Etruscan sculptor they know the name of...'

He shrugged his shoulders, and the gesture expressed a double doubt – doubt whether the archaeologists were right and doubt whether it was really much good talking about Etruscan art to someone who didn't feel quite certain whether the Apollo of Veii was made in the sixth century before or after Christ.

There was a long silence. Fanning looked at the statue. So did Pamela, who also, from time to time, looked at Fanning. She was on the point, more than once, of saying something; but his face was so meditatively glum that, on each occasion, she changed her mind. In the end, however, the silence became intolerable.

'I think it's extraordinarily fine,' she announced in the rather religious voice that seemed appropriate. He only nodded. The silence prolonged itself, more oppressive and embarrassing than ever. She made another and despairing effort.

'Do you know, I think he's really rather like you. I mean, the way he smiles...'

Fanning's petrified immobility broke once more into life. He turned towards her, laughing. 'You're irresistible, Pamela.'

'Am I?' Her tone was cold; she was offended. To be told you were irresistible always meant that you'd behaved like an imbecile child. But her conscience was clear; it was a gratuitous insult

– the more intolerable since it had been offered by the man who, a moment before, had been saying that he had a fellow-feeling for those savages and that her ears had altogether *too* much to do with him.

Fanning noticed her sudden change of humour and obscurely divined the cause.

'You've paid me the most irresistible compliment you could have invented,' he said, doing his best to undo the effect of his words. For after all what did it matter, with little breasts like that and thin brown arms, if she did mix up the millenniums a bit? 'You could hardly have pleased me more if you'd said I was another Rudolph Valentino.'

Pamela had to laugh.

'But seriously,' he said, 'if you knew what this lovely god means to me, how much...'

Mollified by being once more spoken to seriously, 'I think I can understand,' she said in her most understanding voice.

'No, I doubt if you can.' He shook his head. 'It's a question of age, of the experience of a particular time that's not your time. I shall never forget when I came back to Rome for the first time after the war and found this marvellous creature standing here. They only dug him up in 'sixteen, you see. So there it was, a brand new experience, a new and apocalyptic voice out of the past. Some day I shall try to get it on paper, all that this god has taught me.'

He gave a little sigh; she could see that he wasn't thinking about her any more; he was talking for himself. 'Some day,' he repeated. 'But it's not ripe yet. You can't write a thing before it's ripe, before it wants to be written. But you can talk about it, you can take your mind for walks all round it and through it.' He paused and, stretching out a hand, touched a fold of the god's sculptured garment, as though he were trying to establish a more intimate, more real connection with the beauty before him.

'Not that what he taught me was fundamentally new,' he went on slowly. 'It's all in Homer, of course. It's even partially expressed in the archaic Greek sculpture. Partially. But Apollo here expresses it wholly. He's *all* Homer, *all* the ancient world, concentrated in a single lump of terracotta. That's his novelty. And then the circumstances gave him a special point. It was just after the war that I first saw him – just after the apotheosis and the logical conclusion of all the things Apollo *didn't* stand for. You can imagine how marvellously new he seemed by contrast. After that horrible enormity, he was a lovely symbol of the small, the local, the kindly. After all that extravagance of beastliness – yes, and all that extravagance of heroism and self-sacrifice – he seemed so beautifully sane. A god who doesn't admit the separate existence of either heroics or diabolics, but somehow includes them in his own nature and turns them into something else – like two gases combining to make a liquid. Look at him,' Fanning insisted. 'Look at his face, look at his body, see how he stands. It's obvious. He's neither the god of heroics, nor the god of diabolics. And yet it's equally obvious that he knows all about both, that he includes them, that he combines them into a third essence. It's the same with Homer. There's no tragedy in Homer. He's pessimistic, yes; but never tragic. His heroes aren't heroic in our sense of the word; they're men.' (Pamela took a very deep breath; if she had opened her mouth, it would have been a yawn.) 'In fact, you can say there aren't any heroes in Homer. Nor devils, nor sins. And none of our aspiring spiritualities, and, of course, none of our horrible, nauseating disgusts – because they're the complement of being spiritual, they're the tails to its heads. You couldn't have had Homer writing "the expense of spirit in a waste of shame". Though, of course, with Shakespeare, it may have been physiological; the passion violent and brief, and then the most terrible reaction. It's the sort of thing that colours a whole life, a whole work. Only of course one's never allowed to say so. All that one isn't allowed to say!' He laughed. Pamela also laughed.

'But physiology or no physiology,' Fanning went on, 'he couldn't have written like that if he'd lived before the great split – the great split that broke life into spirit and matter, heroics and diabolics, virtue and sin and all the other accursed antitheses. Homer lived before the split; life hadn't been broken when he wrote. They're complete, his men and women, complete and real; for he leaves nothing out, he shirks no issue, even though there is no tragedy. He knows all about it – *all*.' He laid his hand again on the statue. 'And this god's his portrait. He's Homer, but with the Etruscan smile. Homer smiling at the sad, mysterious, beautiful absurdity of the world. The Greeks didn't see that divine absurdity as clearly as the Etruscans. Not even in Homer's day; and by the time you get to any sculptor who was anything like as accomplished as the man who made this, you'll find that they've lost it altogether. True, the earliest Greek gods used to smile all right – or rather grin; for subtlety wasn't their strong point. But by the end of the sixth century they were already becoming a bit too heroic; they were developing those athlete's muscles and those tiresomely noble poses and damned superior faces. But our god here refused to be a prize-fighter or an actor manager. There's no *terribiltà* about him, no priggishness, no sentimentality. And yet without being in the least pretentious, he's beautiful, he's grand, he's authentically divine. The Greeks took the road that led to Michelangelo and Bernini and Thorwaldsen and Rodin. A rake's progress. These Etruscans were on a better track. If only people had had the sense to follow it! Or at least get back to it. But nobody has, except perhaps old Malliol. They've all allowed themselves to be lured away. Plato was the arch-seducer. It was he who first sent us whoring after spirituality and heroics, whoring after the complementary demons of disgust and sin. We needs must love – well, not the highest, except perhaps by accident – but always the most extravagant and exciting. Tragedy was much more exciting than Homer's luminous pessimism, than this God's smiling awareness of the divine absurdity. Being alternately a hero and a sinner is much more sensational than being an integrated man. So as men seem to have the Yellow Press in the blood, like syphilis, they went back on Homer and Apollo; they followed Plato and Euripides. And Plato and Euripides handed them over to the Stoics and the Neo-Platonists. And these in turn handed humanity over to the Christians. And the Christians have handed us over to Henry Ford and the machines. So here we are.'

Pamela nodded intelligently. But what she was chiefly conscious of was the ache in her feet. If only she could sit down! But, 'How poetical and appropriate,' Fanning began again, 'that the god should have risen from the grave exactly when he did, in 1916! Rising up in the midst of the insanity, like a beautiful, smiling reproach from another world. It was dramatic. At least I felt it so, when I saw him just after the war. The resurrection of Apollo, the Etruscan Apollo. I've been his worshipper and self-appointed priest ever since. Or at any rate I've tried to be. But it's difficult.' He shook his head. 'Perhaps it's even impossible for us to recapture...' He left the sentence unfinished and, taking her arm, led her out into the great courtyard of the villa. Under the arcades was a bench. Thank goodness, said Pamela inwardly. They sat down.

'You see,' he went on, leaning forward, his elbows on his knees, his hands clasped, 'you can't get away from the things that the god protests against. Because they've become a part of you. Tradition and education have driven them into your very bones. It's a case of what I was speaking about just now – of the things that have nothing to do with you coming by force of habit to have everything to do with you. Which is why I'd like you to get Apollo and his Etruscans into your system while you're still young. It may save you trouble. Or on the other hand,' he added with a rueful little laugh, 'it may not. Because I really don't know if he's everybody's god. He may do for me – and do, only because I've got Plato and Jesus in my bones. But does he do for you? *Chi lo sa?*[8] The older one grows, the more often one asks that question. Until, of course, one's arteries begin to harden, and then one's opinions begin to harden too, harden till they fossilise into certainty. But meanwhile, *chi lo sa? chi lo sa?* And after all it's quite agreeable, not knowing. And knowing, and at the same time knowing that it's no practical use knowing – that's not disagreeable either. Knowing, for example, that it would be good to live according to this God's commandments, but knowing at the same time that one couldn't do it even if one tried, because one's very guts and skeleton are already pledged to other gods.'

'I should have thought that was awful,' said Pamela.

'For you, perhaps. But I happen to have a certain natural affection for the accomplished fact. I like and respect it, even when it is a bit depressing. Thus, it's a fact that I'd like to think and live in the unsplit, Apollonian way. But it's also a fact – and the fact as such is lovable – that I can't help indulging in aspirations and disgusts; I can't help thinking in terms of heroics and diabolics. Because the division, the splitness, has been worked right into my bones. So has the microbe of sensationalism; I can't help wallowing in the excitements of mysticism and the tragic sense. Can't help it.' He shook his head. 'Though perhaps I've wallowed in them rather more than I was justified in wallowing – justified by my upbringing, I mean. There was a time when I was really quite perversely preoccupied with mystical experiences and ecstasies and private universes.'

'Private universes?' she questioned.

'Yes, private, not shared. You create one, you live in it, each time you're in love, for example.' (Brightly serious, Pamela nodded her understanding and agreement; yes, yes, she knew all about *that*.) 'Each time you're spiritually exalted,' he went on, 'each time you're drunk, even. Everybody has his own favourite short cuts to the other world. Mine, in those days, was opium.'

'Opium?' She opened her eyes very wide. 'Do you mean to say you smoked opium?' She was thrilled. Opium was a vice of the first order.

'It's as good a way of becoming supernatural,' he answered, 'as looking at one's nose or one's navel, or not eating, or repeating a word over and over again, till it loses its sense and you forget how to think. All roads lead to Rome. The only bother about opium is that it's rather an unwholesome road. I had to go to a nursing home in Cannes to get disintoxicated.'

'All the same,' said Pamela, doing her best to imitate the quiet casualness of his manner, 'it must be rather delicious, isn't it? Awfully exciting, I mean,' she added, forgetting not to be thrilled.

'*Too* exciting.' He shook his head. 'That's the trouble. We needs must love the excitingest when we see it. The supernatural *is* exciting. But I don't want to love the supernatural, I want to love the natural. Not that a little supernaturalness isn't, of course, perfectly natural and necessary. But you can overdo it. I overdid it then. I was all the time in t'other world, never here. I stopped smoking because I was ill. But even if I hadn't been, I'd have stopped sooner or later for aesthetic reasons. The supernatural world is so terribly baroque – altogether too Counter-Reformation and Bernini. At its best it can be Greco. But you can have too much even of Greco. A big dose of him makes you begin to pine for Vulca and his Apollo.'

'But doesn't it work the other way too?' she asked. 'I mean, don't you sometimes *long* to start smoking again?' She was secretly hoping he'd let her try a pipe or two.

Fanning shook his head. 'One doesn't get tired of very good bread,' he answered. 'Apollo's like that. I don't pine for supernatural excitements. Which doesn't mean,' he added, 'that I don't in practice run after them. You can't disintoxicate yourself of your culture. That sticks deeper than a mere taste for opium. I'd like to be able to think and live in the spirit of God. But the fact remains that I can't.'

'Can't you?' said Pamela with a polite sympathy. She was more interested in the opium.

'No, no, you can't entirely disintoxicate yourself of mysticism and the tragic sense. You can't take a Turvey treatment for spirituality and disgust. You can't. Not nowadays. Acceptance is impossible in a split world like ours. You've got to recoil. In the circumstances it's right and proper. But absolutely it's wrong. If only one could accept as this god accepts, smiling like that...'

'But you *do* smile like that,' she insisted.

He laughed and, unclasping his hands, straightened himself up in his seat. 'But unhappily,' he said, 'a man can smile and smile and not be Apollo. Meanwhile, what's becoming of your education? Shouldn't we...?'

'Well, if you like,' she assented dubiously. 'Only my feet are rather tired. I mean, there's something about sightseeing...'

'There is indeed,' said Fanning. 'But I was prepared to be a martyr to culture. Still, I'm thankful you're not.' He smiled at her, and Pamela was pleased to find herself once more at the focus of his attention. It had been very interesting to hear him talk about his philosophy and all that. But all the same...

'Twenty to four,' said Fanning, looking at his watch. 'I've an idea; shouldn't we drive out to Monte Cavo and spend the evening up there in the cool? There's a view. And a really very eatable dinner.'

'I'd love to. But...' Pamela hesitated. 'Well, you see I did tell Guy I'd go out with him this evening.'

He was annoyed. 'Well, if you prefer…'

'But I don't prefer,' she answered hastily. 'I mean, I'd much rather go with you. Only I wondered how I'd let Guy know I wasn't…'

'Don't let him know,' Fanning answered, abusing his victory. 'After all, what are young men there for, except to wait when young women don't keep their appointments? It's their function in life.'

Pamela laughed. His word had given her a pleasing sense of importance and power. 'Poor Guy!' she said through her laughter, and her eyes were insolently bright.

'You little hypocrite.'

'I'm not,' she protested. 'I really *am* sorry for him.'

'A little hypocrite *and* a little devil,' was his verdict. He rose to his feet. 'If you could see your own eyes now! But *andiamo*.' He held out his hand to help her up. 'I'm beginning to be rather afraid of you.'

'What nonsense!' She was delighted. They walked together towards the door.

Fanning made the driver go out by the Appian Way. 'For the sake of your education,' he explained, pointing at the ruined tombs, 'which we can continue, thank heaven, in comfort, and at twenty miles an hour.'

Leaning back luxuriously in her corner, Pamela laughed. 'But I must say,' she had to admit, 'it is really rather lovely.'

From Albano the road mounted through the chestnut woods towards Rocca di Papa. A few miles brought them to a turning on the right; the car came to a halt.

'It's barred,' said Pamela, looking out of the window. Fanning had taken out his pocketbook and was hunting among the banknotes and the old letters.

'The road's private,' he explained. 'They ask for your card – heaven knows why. The only trouble being, of course, that I've never possessed such a thing as a visiting card in my life. Still, I generally have one or two belonging to other people. Ah, here we are! Good!' He produced two pieces of pasteboard. A gate-keeper had appeared and was waiting by the door of the car. 'Shall we say we're Count Keyserling?' said Fanning, handing her the Count's card. 'Or alternatively,' he read from the other, 'that we're Herbert Watson, Funeral Furnisher, Funerals conducted with Efficiency and Reverence, Motor Hearses for use in every part of the Country.' He shook his head. 'The last relic of my poor old friend Tom Hatchard. Died last year. I had to bury him. Poor Tom! On the whole I think we'd better be Herbert Watson. *Ecco!*' He handed out the card; the man saluted and went to open the gate. 'But give me back Count Keyserling.' Fanning stretched out his hand. 'He'll come in useful another time.'

The car started and went roaring up the zigzag ascent. Lying back in her corner, Pamela laughed and laughed, inextinguishably.

'But what *is* the joke?' he asked.

She didn't know herself. Mr Watson and the Count had only been a pretext; this enormous laughter, which they had released, sprang from some other, deeper source. And perhaps it was a mere accident that it should be laughter at all. Another pretext, a different finger on the trigger, and it might have been tears, or anger, or singing 'Constantinople' at the top of her voice – anything.

She was limp when they reached the top. Fanning made her sit down where she could see the view and himself went off to order cold drinks at the bar of the little inn that had once been the monastery of Monte Cavo.

Pamela sat where he had left her. The wooded slopes fell steeply away beneath her, down, down to the blue shining of the Alban Lake; and that toy palace perched on the hill beyond was the Pope's, that tiny city in a picture book, Marino. Beyond a dark ridge on the left the round eye of Nemi looked up from its crater. Far off, behind Albano, an expanse of blue steel, burnished beneath the sun, was the Tyrrhenian, and flat like the sea, but golden with ripening corn and powdered goldenly with a haze of dust, the Campagna stretched away from the feet of the subsiding hills, away and up towards a fading horizon, on which the blue ghosts of mountains floated on a level with her eyes. In the midst of the expanse a half-seen golden chaos was Rome. Through the haze the dome of St Peter's shone faintly in the sun with a glitter as of muted glass. There was an enormous silence, sad, sad but somehow consoling. A sacred silence. And yet when, coming up from behind her, Fanning broke it, his voice, for Pamela, committed no iconoclasm; for it seemed, in the world of her feelings, to belong to the silence, it was made, as it were, of the same intimate and friendly substance. He squatted down on his heels beside her, laying a hand on her shoulder to steady himself.

'What a panorama of space and time!' he said. 'So many miles, such an expanse of centuries! You can still walk on the paved road that led to the temple here. The generals used to march up sometimes in triumph. With elephants.'

The silence enveloped them again, bringing them together; and they were alone and as though conspiratorially isolated in an atmosphere of solemn amorousness.

'*I signori son serviti,*' said a slightly ironic voice behind them.

'That's our drinks,' said Fanning. 'Perhaps we'd better...' He got up and, as he unbent them, his knees cracked stiffly. He stooped to rub them, for they ached; his joints were old. 'Fool!' he said to himself, and decided that tomorrow he'd go to Venice. She was too young, too dangerously and perversely fresh.

They drank their lemonade in silence. Pamela's face wore an expression of grave serenity which it touched and flattered and moved him to see. Still, he was a fool to be touched and flattered and moved.

'Let's go for a bit of a stroll,' he said, when they had slaked their thirst. She got up without a word, obediently, as though she had become his slave.

It was breathless under the trees and there was a smell of damp, hot greenness, a hum and flicker of insects in the probing slants of sunlight. But in the open spaces the air of the heights was quick and nimble, in spite of the sun; the broom-flower blazed among the rocks; and round the bushes where the honey-suckle had clambered, there hung invisible islands of perfume, cool and fresh in the midst of the hot sea of bracken smell. Pamela moved here and there with little exclamations of delight, pulling at the tough sprays of honeysuckle.

'Oh, look!' she called to him in her rapturous voice. 'Come and look!'

'I'm looking,' he shouted back across the intervening space. 'With a telescope. With the eye of faith,' he corrected; for she had moved out of sight. He sat down on a smooth rock and lighted a cigarette. Venice, he reflected, would be rather boring at this particular season. In a few minutes Pamela came back to him, flushed, with a great bunch of honeysuckle between her hands.

'You know, you ought to have come,' she said reproachfully. 'There were such *lovely* pieces I couldn't reach.'

Fanning shook his head. 'He also serves who only sits and smokes,' he said, and made room for her on the stone beside him. 'And what's more,' he went on, '"let Austin have his swink to him reserved". Yes, let him. How wholeheartedly I've always agreed with Chaucer's Monk! Besides, you seem to forget, my child, that I'm an old, old gentleman.' He was playing the safe, prudent part. Perhaps if he played it hard enough, it wouldn't be necessary to go to Venice.

Pamela paid no attention to what he was saying. 'Would you like this one for your buttonhole, Miles?' she asked, holding up a many-trumpeted flower. It was the first time she had called him by his Christian name, and the accomplishment of this much-meditated act of daring made her blush. 'I'll stick it in,' she added, leaning forward, so that he shouldn't see her reddened cheeks, till her face was almost touching his coat. Near and thus offered (for it was an offer, he had no doubt of that, a deliberate offer) why shouldn't he take this lovely, this terribly and desperately tempting freshness? It was a matter of stretching out one's hands. But no; it would be too insane. She was near, this warm young flesh, this scent of her hair, near and offered – with what an innocent perversity, what a touchingly ingenuous and uncomprehending shamelessness! But he sat woodenly still, feeling all of a sudden as he had felt when, a lanky boy, he had been too shy, too utterly terrified, in spite of his longings, to kiss that Jenny – what on earth was her name? – that Jenny Something-or-Other he had danced the polka with at Uncle Fred's one Christmas, how many centuries ago! – and yet only yesterday, only this instant.

'There!' said Pamela, and drew back. Her cheeks had had time to cool a little.

'Thank you.' There was a silence.

'Do you know,' she said at last, efficiently, 'you've got a button loose on your coat.'

He fingered the hanging button. 'What a damning proof of celibacy!'

'If only I had a needle and thread…'

'Don't make your offer too lightly. If you knew what a quantity of unmended stuff I've got at home…'

'I'll come and do it tomorrow,' she promised, feeling delightfully protective and important.

'Beware,' he said. 'I'll take you at your word. It's sweated labour.'

'I don't mind. I'll come.'

'Punctually at ten-thirty, then.' He had forgotten about Venice. 'I shall be a ruthless taskmaster.'

Nemi was already in shadow when they walked back; but the higher slopes were transfigured with the setting sunlight. Pamela halted at a twist of the path and turned back towards the western sky. Looking up, Fanning saw her standing there, goldenly flushed, the colours of her skin, her hair, her dress, the flowers in her hands, supernaturally heightened and intensified in the almost level light.

'I think this is the most lovely place I've ever seen.' Her voice was solemn with a natural piety. 'But you're not looking,' she added in a different tone, reproachfully.

'I'm looking at you,' he answered. After all, if he stopped in time, it didn't matter his behaving like a fool – it didn't finally matter and, meanwhile, was very agreeable.

An expression of impertinent mischief chased away the solemnity from her face. 'Trying to see my ears again?' she asked; and, breaking off a honeysuckle blossom, she threw it down in his face, then turned and ran up the steep path.

'Don't imagine I'm going to pursue,' he called after her. 'The Pan and Syrinx business is a winter pastime. Like football.'

Her laughter came down to him from among the trees; he followed the retreating sound. Pamela waited for him at the top of the hill and they walked back together towards the inn.

'Aren't there any ruins here?' she asked. 'I mean, for my education.'

He shook his head. 'The Young Pretender's brother pulled them all down and built a monastery with them. For the Passionist Fathers,' he added after a little pause. 'I feel rather like a Passionist Father myself at the moment.' They walked on without speaking, enveloped by the huge, the amorously significant silence.

But a few minutes later, at the dinner table, they were exuberantly gay. The food was well cooked, the wine an admirable Falernian. Fanning began to talk about his early loves. Vaguely at first, but later, under Pamela's questioning, with an ever-increasing wealth of specific detail. They were indiscreet, impudent questions, which at ordinary times she couldn't have uttered, or at least have only despairingly forced out, with a suicide's determination. But she was a little tipsy now, tipsy with the wine and her own laughing exultation; she rapped them out easily, without a tremor. 'As though you were the immortal Sigmund himself,' he assured her, laughing. Her impudence and that knowledgeable, scientific ingenuousness amused him, rather perversely; he told her everything she asked.

When she had finished with his early loves, she questioned him about the opium. Fanning described his private universes and that charming nurse who had looked after him while he was being disintoxicated. He went on to talk about the black poverty he'd been reduced to by the drug. 'Because you can't do journalism or write novels in the other world,' he explained. 'At least I never could.' And he told her of the debts he still owed and of his present arrangements with his publishers.

Almost suddenly the night was cold and Fanning became aware that the bottle had been empty for a long time. He threw away the stump of his cigar. 'Let's go.' They took their seats and the car set off, carrying with it the narrow world of form and colour created by its headlamps. They were alone in the darkness of their padded box. An hour before, Fanning had decided that he would take this opportunity to kiss her. But he was haunted suddenly by the memory of an Australian who had once complained to him of the sufferings of a young colonial in England. 'In Sydney,' he had said, 'when I get into a taxi with a nice girl, I know exactly what to do. And I know exactly what to do when I'm in an American taxi. But when I apply my knowledge in London – God, isn't there a row!' How vulgar and stupid it all was! Not merely a fool, but a vulgar, stupid fool. He sat unmoving in his corner. When the lights of Rome were round them, he took her hand and kissed it.

'Goodnight.'

She thanked him. 'I've had the loveliest day.' But her eyes were puzzled and unhappy. Meeting them, Fanning suddenly regretted his self-restraint, wished that he had been stupid and vulgar. And, after all, would it have been so stupid and vulgar? You could make any action seem anything you liked, from saintly to disgusting, by describing it in the appropriate words. But his regrets had come too late. Here was her hotel. He drove home to his solitude feeling exceedingly depressed.

6

June 14th. Spent the morning with M., who lives in a house belonging to a friend of his who is a Catholic and lives in Rome, M. says, because he likes to get his popery straight from the horse's mouth. A nice house, old, standing just back from the Forum, which I said I thought was like a rubbish heap and he agreed with me, in spite of my education, and said he always preferred live dogs to dead lions and thinks it's awful the way the Fascists are pulling down nice ordinary houses and making holes to find more of these beastly pillars and things. I sewed on a lot of buttons, etc., as he's living in only two rooms on the ground floor and the servants are on their holiday, so he eats out and an old woman comes to clean up in the afternoons, but doesn't do any mending, which meant a lot for me, but I liked doing it, in spite of the darning, because he sat with me all the time, sometimes talking, sometimes just working. When he's writing or sitting with his pen in his hand thinking, his face is quite still and *terribly* serious and far, far away, as though he were a picture, or more like some sort of not-human person, a sort of angel, if one can imagine them without nightdresses and long hair, really rather frightening, so that one longed to shout or throw a reel of cotton at him so as to change him back again into a man. He has very beautiful hands, rather long and bony, but strong. Sometimes, after he'd sat thinking for a long time, he'd get up and walk about the room, frowning and looking kind of angry, which was still more terrifying – sitting there while he walked up and down quite close to me, as though he were absolutely alone. But one time he suddenly stopped his walking up and down and said how profusely he apologised for his toes, because I was darning, and it was really wonderful to see him suddenly changed back from that picture-angel sort of creature into a human being. Then he sat down by me and said he'd been spending the morning wrestling with the problem of speaking the truth in books; so I said, but haven't you always spoken it? Because that always seemed to me the chief point of M.'s books. But he said, not much, because most of it was quite unspeakable in our world, as we found it too shocking and humiliating. So I said, all the same I didn't see why it shouldn't be spoken, and he said, nor did he in theory, but in practice he didn't want to be lynched. And he said, look for example at those advertisements in American magazines with the photos and life stories of people with unpleasant breath. So I said, yes, aren't they simply *too* awful. Because they really do make one shudder. And he said, precisely, there you are, and they're so successful because everyone thinks them so perfectly awful. They're outraged by them, he said, just as you're outraged, and they rush off and buy stuff in sheer terror, because they're so terrified of being an outrage physically to other people. And he said, that's only one small sample of all the class of truths, pleasant and unpleasant, that you can't speak, except in scientific books, but that doesn't count, because you deliberately leave your feelings outside in the cloakroom when you're being scientific. And just because they're unspeakable, we pretend they're unimportant, but they aren't, on the contrary, they're terribly important, and he said, you've only got to examine your memory quite sincerely for five minutes to realise it, and of course he's quite right. When I think of Miss Poole giving me piano lessons – but no, really, one *can't* write these things, and yet one obviously ought to, because they *are* so important, the humiliating physical facts, both pleasant and unpleasant (though I must say, most of the ones I can think of seem to be unpleasant), so important in all human relationships, he says, even in love, which is really rather awful, but of course one must admit it. And M. said it would take a whole generation of being shocked and humiliated and lynching the shockers and humiliators before people could settle down to listening to that sort of truth calmly, which they did do, he says, at certain times in the past, at any rate much more so than now. And he says that when they can listen to it completely calmly, the world will be quite different from what it is now, so I asked, in what way? but he said he couldn't clearly imagine, only he knew it would be different. After that he went back to his table and wrote very quickly for about half an hour without stopping, and I longed to ask him if he'd been writing the truth, and if so, what about, but I didn't have the nerve, which was stupid.

We lunched at our usual place, which I really don't much like, as who wants to look at fat businessmen and farmers from the country simply *drinking* spaghetti? Even if the spaghetti *is* good, but M. prefers it to the big places, because he says that in Rome one must do as the Romans do, not as the Americans. Still, I must say I do like looking at people who dress well and have good manners and nice jewels and things, which I told him, so he said all right, we'd go to Valadier's tomorrow to see how the rich ate macaroni, which made me wretched, as it looked as though I'd been cadging, and of course that's the last thing in the world I meant to do, to make him waste a lot of money on me, particularly after what he told me yesterday about his debts and what he made on the average, which still seems to me shockingly little, considering who he is, so I said no, wouldn't he lunch with *me* at Valadier's, and he laughed and said it was the first time he'd heard of a gigolo of fifty being taken out by a woman of twenty. That rather upset me – the way it seemed to bring what we are to each other on to the wrong level, making it all a sort of joke and sniggery, like something in *Punch*. Which is hateful, I can't bear it. And I have the feeling that he does it on purpose, as a kind of protection, because he doesn't want to care too much, and that's why he's always saying he's so old, which is all nonsense, because you're only as old as you feel, and sometimes I even feel older than he does, like when he gets so amused and interested with little boys in the street playing that game of sticking out your fingers and calling a number, or when he talks about that awful old Dickens. Which I told him, but he only laughed and said age is a circle and you grow into a lot of the things you grew out of, because the whole world is a fried whiting with its tail in its mouth, which only confirms what I said about his saying he was old being all nonsense. Which I told him and he said, quite right, he only *said* he felt old when he *wished* that he felt old. Which made me see still more clearly that it was just a defence. A defence of *me*, I suppose, and all that sort of nonsense.

What I'd have liked to say, only I didn't, was that I don't want to be defended, particularly if being defended means his defending himself against me and making stupid jokes about gigolos and old gentlemen. Because I think he really does rather care underneath – from the way he looks at me sometimes – and he'd like to say so and act so, but he won't on principle, which is really against all *his* principles, and some time I *shall* tell him so. I insisted he should lunch with me and in the end he said he would, and then he was suddenly very silent and, I thought, glum and unhappy, and after coffee he said he'd have to go home and write all the rest of the day. So I came back to the hotel and had a rest and wrote this, and now it's nearly seven and I feel terribly sad, almost like crying.

Next day. Rang up Guy and had less difficulty than I expected getting him to forgive me for yesterday, in fact he almost apologised himself. Danced till 2.15.

June 15th. M. still sad and didn't kiss me when we met, *on purpose*, which made me angry, it's so humiliating to be defended. He was wearing an open shirt, like Byron, which suited him; but I told him, you look like the devil when you're sad (which is true, because his face ought to move, not be still), and he said that was what came of feeling and behaving like an angel; so of course I asked why he didn't behave like a devil, because in that case he'd look like an angel, and I preferred his looks to his morals, and then I blushed, like an idiot. But really it is too stupid that women aren't supposed to say what they think. Why can't we say, I like you, or whatever it is, without being thought a kind of monster, if we say it first, and even thinking ourselves monsters? Because one ought to say what one thinks and do what one likes, or else one becomes like Aunt Edith, hippo-ish and dead inside. Which is after all what M.'s constantly saying in his books, so he oughtn't to humiliate me with his beastly defendings.

Lunch at Valadier's was really rather a bore. Afterwards we went and sat in a church, because it was so hot, a huge affair full of pink marble and frescoes and marble babies and gold. M. says that the modern equivalent is Lyons' Corner House, and that the Jesuits were so successful because they gave the poor a chance of feeling what it was like to live in a palace, or something better than a palace, because he says the chief difference between a Corner House and the state rooms at Buckingham Palace is that the Corner House is so much more sumptuous, almost as sumptuous as these Jesuit churches. I asked him if he believed in God and he said he believed in a great many gods, it depended on what he was doing, or being, or feeling at the moment. He said he believed in Apollo when he was working, and in Bacchus when he was drinking, and in Buddha when he felt depressed, and in Venus when he was making love, and in the Devil when he was afraid or angry, and in the Categorical Imperative when he had to do his duty. I asked him which he believed in now and he said he didn't quite know, but he thought it was the Categorical Imperative, which really made me furious, so I answered that I only believed in the Devil and Venus, which made him laugh, and he said I looked as though

I were going to jump off the Eiffel Tower, and I was just going to say what I thought of his hippo-ishness, I mean I'd really made up my mind, when a most horrible old verger rushed up and said we must leave the church, because it seems the Pope doesn't allow you to be in a church with bare arms, which is really *too* indecent. But M. said that after all it wasn't surprising, because every god has to protect himself against hostile gods, and the gods of bare skin *are* hostile to the gods of souls and clothes, and he made me stop in front of a shop window where there were some mirrors and said, you can see for yourself, and I must say I really did look very nice in that pale green linen which goes so awfully well with the skin, when one's a bit sunburnt. But he said, it's not merely a question of seeing, you must touch too, so I stroked my arms and said yes, they were nice and smooth, and he said, precisely, and then he stroked my arm very lightly, like a moth crawling, agonisingly creepy but delicious, once or twice, looking very serious and attentive, as though he were tuning a piano, which made me laugh, and I said I supposed he was experimenting to see if the Pope was in the right, and then he gave me the most horrible pinch and said, yes, the Pope was quite right and I ought to be muffled in Jaegar from top to toe. But I was so angry with the pain, because he pinched me really terribly, that I just rushed off without saying anything and jumped into a cab that was passing and drove straight to the hotel. But I was so wretched by the time I got there that I started crying in the lift and the lift man said he hoped I hadn't had any *dispiacere di famiglia*,[9] which made me laugh and that made the crying much worse, and then I suddenly thought of Clare and felt such a horrible beast, so I lay on my bed and simply howled for about an hour, and then I got up and wrote a letter and sent one of the hotel boys with it to M.'s address, saying I was so sorry and would he come at once. But he didn't come, not for hours and hours, and it was simply too awful, because I thought he was offended, or despising, because I'd been such a fool, and I wondered whether he really did like me at all and whether this defending theory wasn't just my imagination. But at last, when I'd quite given him up and was so miserable I didn't know what I should do, he suddenly appeared – because he'd only that moment gone back to the house and found my note – and was too wonderfully sweet to me, and said he was so sorry, but he'd been on edge (though he didn't say why, but I know now that the defending theory wasn't just imagination) and I said I was so sorry and I cried, but I was happy, and then we laughed because it had all been so stupid and then M. quoted a bit of Homer which meant that after they'd eaten and drunk they wept for their friends and after they'd wept a little they went to sleep, so we went out and had dinner and after dinner we went and danced, and he dances really very well, but we stopped before midnight, because he said the noise of the jazz would drive him crazy. He was perfectly sweet, but though he didn't say anything sniggery, I could feel he was on the defensive all the time, sweetly and friendlily on the defensive, and when he said goodnight he only kissed my hand.

June 18th. Stayed in bed till lunch rereading *The Return of Eurydice*. I understand Joan so well now, better and better, she's *so* like me in all she feels and thinks. M. went to Tivoli for the day to see some Italian friends who have a house there. What is he like with other people? I wonder. Got two tickets for the fireworks tomorrow night, the hotel porter says they'll be good, because it's the first Girandola since the war. Went to the Villa Borghese in the afternoon for my education, to give M. a surprise when he comes back, and I must say some of the pictures and statues were very lovely, but the most awful-looking fat man would follow me round all the time, and finally the old beast even had the impertinence to speak to me, so I just said, *Lei è un porco*,[10] which I must say was very effective. But it's extraordinary how things do just depend on looks and being sympathique, because if he hadn't looked such a pig, I shouldn't have thought him so piggish, which shows again what rot hippo-ism is. Went to bed early and finished *Eurydice*. This is the fifth time I've read it.

7

'Oh, it was marvellous before the war, the Girandola. Really marvellous.'

'But then what wasn't *marvellous* before the war?' said Pamela sarcastically. These references to a Golden Age in which she had had no part always annoyed her.

Fanning laughed. 'Another one in the eye for the aged gentleman!'

There, he had slipped back again behind his defences! She did not answer for fear of giving him some excuse to dig himself in, impregnably. This hateful bantering with feelings! They walked on in silence. The night was breathlessly warm; the sounds of brassy music came to them faintly through the dim enormous noise of a crowd that thickened with every step they took towards the Piazza del Popolo. In the end they had to shove their way by main force.

Sunk head over ears in this vast sea of animal contacts, animal smells and noise, Pamela was afraid. 'Isn't it awful?' she said, looking up at him over her shoulder; and she shuddered. But at the same time she rather liked her fear, because it seemed in some way to break down the barriers that separated them, to bring him closer to her – close with a physical closeness of protective contact that was also, increasingly, a closeness of thought and feeling. 'You're all right,' he reassured her through the tumult. He was standing behind her, encircling her with his arms. 'I won't let you be squashed'; and as he spoke he fended off the menacing lurch of a large back. '*Ignorante!*' he shouted at it. A terrific explosion interrupted the distant selections from *Rigoletto* and the sky was suddenly full of coloured lights; the Girandola had begun. A wave of impatience ran through the advancing crowd; they were violently pushed and jostled. But, 'It's all right,' Fanning kept repeating, 'it's all right.'

They were squeezed together in a staggering embrace. Pamela was terrified, but it was with a kind of swooning pleasure that she shut her eyes and abandoned herself limply in his arms.

'*Ma piano!*' shouted Fanning at the nearest jostlers. '*Piano!*' and "Sblood!' he said in English, for he had the affectation of using literary oaths. 'Hell and Death!' But in the tumult his words were as though unspoken. He was silent; and suddenly, in the midst of that heaving chaos of noise and rough contacts, of movement and heat and smell, suddenly he became aware that his lips were almost touching her hair, and that under his right hand was the firm resilience of her breast. He hesitated for a moment on the threshold of his sensuality, then averted his face, shifted the position of his hand.

'At last!' The haven to which their tickets admitted them was a little garden on the western side of the Piazza, opposite the Pincio and the source of the fireworks. The place was crowded, but not oppressively. Fanning was tall enough to overlook the interposed heads, and when Pamela had climbed on to a little parapet that separated one terrace of the garden from another, she too could see perfectly.

'But you'll let me lean on you,' she said, laying a hand on his shoulder, 'because there's a fat woman next to me who's steadily squeezing me off. I think she's expanding with the heat.'

'And she almost certainly understands English. So for heaven's sake…'

A fresh volley of explosions from the other side of the great square interrupted him and drowned the answering mockery of her laughter. 'Ooh! ooh!' the crowd was moaning in a kind of amorous agony. Magical flowers in a delirium of growth, the rockets mounted on their slender stalks and, 'ah!' high up above the Pincian hill, dazzlingly, deafeningly, in a bunch of stars and a thunderclap, they blossomed.

'Isn't it marvellous?' said Pamela, looking down at him

with shining eyes. 'Oh God!' she added, in another voice. 'She's expanding again. Help!' And for a moment she was on the verge of falling. She leaned on him so heavily that he had to make an effort not to be pushed sideways. She managed to straighten herself up again into equilibrium.

'I've got you in case...' He put his arms round her knees to steady her.

'Shall I see if I can puncture the old beast with a pin?'

And Fanning knew, by the tone of her voice, that she was genuinely prepared to make the experiment.

'If you do,' he said, 'I shall leave you to be lynched alone.'

Pamela felt his arm tighten a little about her thighs. 'Coward!' she mocked and pulled his hair.

'Martyrdom's not in my line,' he laughed back. 'Not even martyrdom for your sake.'

But her youth was a perversity, her freshness a kind of provocative vice. He had taken a step across that supernatural threshold. He had given – after all, why not? – a certain licence to his desires. Amid their multitudinous uncoiling, his body seemed to be coming to a new and obscure life of its own. When the time came he would revoke the licence, step back again into the daily world.

There was another bang, another, and the obelisk at the centre of the Piazza leapt out sharp and black against apocalypse after apocalypse of jewelled light. And through the now flushed, now pearly-brilliant, now emerald-shining smoke-clouds, a pine tree, a palm, a stretch of grass emerged, like strange unearthly visions of pine and palm and grass, from the darkness of the else invisible gardens.

There was an interval of mere lamplight – like sobriety, said Fanning, between two pipes of opium, like daily life after an ecstasy. And perhaps, he was thinking, the time to step back again had already come.

'If only one could live without any lucid intervals,' he concluded.

'I don't see why not.' She spoke with a kind of provocative defiance, as though challenging him to contradict her. Her heart beat very fast, exultantly. 'I mean, why shouldn't it be fireworks all the time?'

'Because it just isn't, that's all. Unhappily.' It was time to step back again; but he didn't step back.

'Well, then, it's a case of damn the intervals and enjoy... Oh!' She started. That prodigious bang had sent a large red moon sailing almost slowly into the sky. It burst into a shower of meteors that whistled as they fell, expiringly.

Fanning imitated their plaintive noise. 'Sad, sad,' he commented. 'Even the fireworks can be sad.'

She turned on him fiercely. 'Only because you want them to be sad. Yes, you want them to be. Why do you want them to be sad?'

Yes, why? It was a pertinent question. She felt his arm tighten again round her knees and was triumphant. He was defending himself no more, he was listening to those oracles. But at the root of his deliberate recklessness, its contradiction and its cause, his sadness obscurely persisted.

'But I *don't* want them to be sad,' he protested.

Another garden of rockets began to blossom. Laughing, triumphant, Pamela laid her hand on his head.

'I feel so superior up here,' she said.

'On a pedestal, what?' He laughed. '*Guardami ben; ben son, ben son Beatrice!*'[11]

'Such a comfort you're not bald,' she said, her fingers in his hair. 'That must be a great disadvantage of pedestals – I mean, seeing the baldness of the men down below.'

'But the great advantage of pedestals, as I now suddenly see for the first time...' Another explosion covered his voice. '...make it possible...' Bang!

'Oh, look!' A bluish light was brightening, brightening.

'… possible for even the baldest…' There was a continuous uninterrupted rattle of detonations. Fanning gave it up. What he had meant to say was that pedestals gave even the baldest men unrivalled opportunities for pinching the idol's legs.

'What were you saying?' she shouted through the battle.

'Nothing,' he yelled back.

He had meant, of course, to suit the action to the word, playfully. But the fates had decided otherwise and he wasn't really sorry. For he was tired; he had realised it almost suddenly. All this standing. He was no good at standing nowadays.

A cataract of silver fire was pouring down the slopes of the Pincian hill, and the shining smoke-clouds rolled away from it like the spray from a tumbling river. And suddenly, above it, the eagle of Savoy emerged from the darkness, enormous, perched on the lictor's axe and rods. There was applause and patriotic music. Then, gradually, the brightness of the cataract grew dim; the sources of its silver streaming were one by one dried up. The eagle moulted its shining plumage, the axe and rods faded, faded and at last were gone. Lit faintly by only the common lamplight, the smoke drifted slowly away towards the north. A spasm of motion ran through the huge crowd in the square below them. The show was over.

'But I feel,' said Pamela, as they shoved their way back towards the open streets, 'I feel as though the rockets were still popping off inside me.' And she began to sing to herself as she walked. Fanning made no comment. He was thinking of that Girandola he'd seen with Alice and Tony and Laurina Frescobaldi – was it in 1907 or 1908? Tony was an ambassador now, and Alice was dead, and one of Laurina's sons (he recalled the expression of despair on that worn, but still handsome face, when she had told him yesterday, at Tivoli) was already old enough to be getting housemaids into trouble.

'Not only rockets,' Pamela went on, interrupting her singing, 'but even Catherine wheels. I feel all Catherine-wheely. You know, like when one's a little drunk.' And she went on again with 'Old Man River', tipsily happy and excited.

The crowd grew thinner around them and at last they were almost alone. Pamela's singing abruptly ceased. Here, in the open, in the cool of the dark night it had suddenly become inappropriate, a little shameful. She glanced anxiously at her companion; had he too remarked that inappropriateness, been shocked by it? But Fanning had noticed nothing; she wished he had. Head bent, his hands behind his back, he was walking at her side, but in another universe. When had his spirit gone away from her, and why? She didn't know, hadn't noticed. Those inward fireworks, that private festival of exultation had occupied her whole attention. She had been too excitedly happy with being in love to be able to think of the object of that love. But now, abruptly sobered, she had become aware of him again, repentantly at first, and then, as she realised his new remoteness, with a sinking of the heart. What had happened in these few moments? She was on the point of addressing him, then checked herself. Her apprehension grew and grew till it became a kind of terrified certainty that he'd never loved her at all, that he'd suddenly begun to hate her. But why, but why? They walked on.

'How lovely it is here!' she said at last. Her voice was timid and unnatural. 'And so deliciously cool.' They had emerged on to the embankment of the Tiber. Above the river, a second invisible river of air flowed softly through the hot night. 'Shall we stop for a moment?' He nodded without speaking. 'I mean, only if you want to,' she added. He nodded again. They stood, leaning on the parapet, looking down at the black water. There was a long, long silence. Pamela waited for him to say something, to make a gesture; but he did not stir, the word never came. It was as though he were at the other end of the world. She felt almost sick with unhappiness. Heartbeat after heartbeat, the silence prolonged itself.

Fanning was thinking of tomorrow's journey. How he hated the train! And in this heat... But it was necessary. The wicked flee, and in this case the fleeing would be an act of virtue – painful. Was it love? Or just an itch of desire, of the rather crazy, dirty desire of an ageing man?

'*A cinquant' anni si diventa un po' pazzo.*'[12] He heard his own voice speaking, laughing, mournfully, to Laurina. '*Pazzo e porco. Si, anch' io divento un porco. Le minorenni – a cinquant' anni, sa, sono un ossessione. Proprio un' ossessione.*'[13]

Was that all – just an obsession of crazy desire? Or what is love? Or wasn't there any difference, was it just a question of names and approving or disapproving tones of voice? What was certain was that you could be as desperately unhappy when you were robbed of your crazy desire as when you were robbed of your love. A *porco* suffers as much as Dante. And perhaps Beatrice too was lovely, in Dante's memory, with the perversity of youth, the shamelessness of innocence, the vice of freshness. Still, the wicked flee, the wicked flee. If only he'd had the strength of mind to flee before! A touch made him start. Pamela had taken his hand.

'Miles!' Her voice was strained and abnormal. Fanning turned towards her and was almost frightened by the look of determined despair he saw on her face. The Eiffel Tower... 'Miles!'

'What is it?'

'Why don't you speak to me?'

He shrugged his shoulders.

'I didn't happen to be feeling very loquacious. For a change,' he added, self-mockingly, in the hope (he knew it for a vain one) of being able to turn away her desperate attack with a counter-attack of laughter.

She ignored his counter-attack. 'Why do you shut yourself away from me like this?' she asked. 'Why do you hate me?'

'But my sweet child...'

'Yes, you hate me. You shut me away. Why are you so cruel, Miles?' Her voice broke; she was crying. Lifting his hand, she kissed it, passionately, despairingly. 'I love you so much, Miles, I love you.'

His hand was wet with tears when, almost by force, he managed to draw it away from her. He put his arm around her, comfortingly. But he was annoyed as well as touched, annoyed by her despairing determination, by the way she had made up her mind to jump off the Eiffel Tower, screwed up her courage turn by turn. And now she was jumping – but how gracelessly! The way he positively had to struggle for his hand! There was something forced and unnatural about the whole scene. She was being a character in fiction. But characters in fiction suffer. He patted her shoulder, he made consolatory murmurs. Consoling her for being in love with him! But the idea of explaining and protesting and being lucidly reasonable was appalling to him at the moment, absolutely appalling. He hoped that she'd just permit herself to be consoled and ask no further questions, just leave the whole situation comfortably inarticulate. But his hope was again disappointed.

'Why do you hate me, Miles?' she insisted.

'But, Pamela...'

'Because you did care a little, you did. I mean, I could see you cared. And now, suddenly... What have I done, Miles?'

'But nothing, my child, nothing.' He could not keep a note of exasperation out of his voice. If only she'd allow him to be silent!

'Nothing? But I can hear from the way you speak that there's something.' She returned to her old refrain. 'Because you did care, Miles; a little, you did.' She looked up at him, but he moved away from her, he had averted his eyes towards the street. 'You did, Miles.'

Oh God! he was groaning to himself, God! And aloud (for she had made his silence untenable, she had driven him out into articulateness), 'I cared too much,' he said. 'It would be so easy to do something stupid and irreparable, something mad, yes and bad, bad. I like you too much in other ways to want to run that risk. Perhaps, if I were twenty years younger... But I'm too old. It wouldn't do. And you're too young, you can't really understand, you... Oh, thank God, there's a taxi.' And he darted forward, waving and shouting. Saved! But when they had shut themselves into the cab, he found that the new situation was even more perilous than the old.

'Miles!' A flash of lamplight through the window of the cab revealed her face to him. His words had consoled her; she was smiling, was trying to look happy; but under the attempted happiness her expression was more desperately determined than ever. She was not yet at the bottom of her tower. 'Miles!' And sliding across the seat towards him, she threw her arms round his neck and kissed him. 'Take me, Miles,' she said, speaking in quick abrupt little spurts, as though she were forcing the words out with violence against a resistance. He recognised the suicide's voice, despairing, strained, and at the same time, flat, lifeless. 'Take me. If you want me...'

Fanning tried to protest, to disengage himself, gently, from her embrace. 'But I want you to take me, Miles,' she insisted. 'I want you...' She kissed him again, she pressed herself against his hard body. 'I want you, Miles. Even if it is stupid and mad,' she added in another little spurt of desperation, making answer to the expression on his face, to the words she wouldn't permit him to utter. 'And it isn't. I mean, love isn't stupid or mad. Even if it were, I don't care. Yes, I want to be stupid and mad. Even if it were to kill me. So take me, Miles.' She kissed him again. 'Take me.'

He turned away his mouth from those soft lips. She was forcing him back across the threshold. His body was uneasy with awakenings and supernatural dawn.

Held up by a tram at the corner of a narrow street, the cab was at a standstill. With quick strong gestures Fanning unclasped her arms from round his neck and, taking her two hands in his, he kissed first one and then the other. 'Goodbye, Pamela,' he whispered, and, throwing open the door, he was half out of the cab before she realised what he was doing.

'But what are you doing, Miles? Where…'

The door slammed. He thrust some money into the driver's hand and almost ran. Pamela rose to her feet to follow him, but the cab started with a sudden jerk that threw her off her balance, and she fell back on to the seat. 'Miles!' she called, and then, 'Stop!' But the driver either didn't hear, or else paid no attention. She did not call again, but sat, covering her face with her hands, crying and feeling so agonisingly unhappy that she thought she would die of it.

8

'By the time you receive this letter, I shall be – no, not dead, Pamela, though I know how thrilled and proud you'd be, through your temporary inconsolability, if I were to blow my brains out – not dead, but (what will be almost worse in these dog-days) in the train, bound for some anonymous refuge. Yes, a refuge, as though you were my worst enemy. Which in fact you almost are at the moment, for the good reason that you're acting as your own enemy. If I were less fond of you, I'd stay and join forces with you against yourself. And, frankly, I wish I were less fond of you. Do you know how desirable you are? Not yet, I suppose, not consciously, in spite of Prof. Krafft-Ebbing and the novels of Miles F. You can't yet know what a terrible army with banners you are, you and your eyes and your laughter and your impertinent breasts, like La Maja's, and those anti-educational ears in ambush under the hair. You can't know. But I know. Only too well. Just *how* well you'll realise, perhaps, fifteen or twenty years from now. For a time will come when the freshness of young bodies, the ingenuousness of young minds will begin to strike you as a scandal of shining beauty and attractiveness, and then finally as a kind of maddeningly alluring perversity, as the exhibition of a kind of irresistibly dangerous vice. The madness of the desirer – for middle-aged desires are mostly more or less mad desires – comes off on the desired object, staining it, degrading it. Which isn't agreeable if you happen to be fond of the object, as well as desiring. Dear object, let's be a little reasonable – oh, entirely against all my principles; I accept all the reproaches you made me the other day. But what are principles for but to be gone against in moments of crisis? And this *is* a moment of crisis. Consider: I'm thirty years older than you are; and even if one doesn't look one's age, one is one's age, somehow, somewhere;

and even if one doesn't feel it, fifty's always fifty and twenty-one's twenty-one. And when you've considered that, let me put a few questions. First: are you prepared to be a disreputable woman? To which, of course, you answer yes, because you don't care two pins about what the old cats say. But I put another question: Do you know, by experience, what it's like to be a disreputable woman? And you must answer, no. Whereupon I retort: If you can't answer yes to the second, you've no right to answer yes to the first. And I don't intend to give you the opportunity of answering yes to the second question. Which is all pure Podsnapism.[14] But there are certain circumstances in which Podsnap is quite right.

'Sweet Pamela, believe me when I say it would be fatal. For when you say you love me, what do you mean? Who and what is it you love? I'll tell you. You love the author of *Eurydice* and of all those portraits of yourself he's filled his books with. You love the celebrated man, who was not only unsnubbing and attentive, but obviously admiring. Even before you saw him, you vaguely loved his reputation, and now you love his odd confidences. You love a kind of conversation you haven't heard before. You love a weakness in him which you think you can dominate and protect. You love – as I, of course, intended you to love – a certain fascinating manner. You even love a rather romantic and still youthful appearance. And when I say (which as yet, you know, I haven't said) that I love you, what do *I* mean? That I'm amused, and charmed, and flattered, and touched, and puzzled, and affectionate, in a word, a Passionist Father. But chiefly that I find you terribly desirable – an army with banners. Bring these two loves together and what's the result? A manifold disaster. To begin with, the nearer you come to me and the longer you remain with me, the more alien you'll find me, the more fundamentally remote. Inevitably. For you and I are foreigners to one another, foreigners in time.

Which is a greater foreignness than the foreignness of space and language. You don't realise it now, because you don't know me – you're only in love, at first sight (like Joan in *Eurydice* !) and, what's more, not really with me, with your imagination of me. When you come to know me better – well, you'll find that you know me much worse. And then one day you'll be attracted by a temporal compatriot. Perhaps, indeed, you're attracted already, only your imagination won't allow you to admit it. What about that long-suffering Guy of yours? Of whom I was, and am, so horribly jealous – jealous with the malignity of a weaker for a stronger rival; for though I seem to hold all the cards at the moment, the ace of trumps is his: he's young. And one day, when you're tired of living at cross-purposes with me, you'll suddenly realise it; you'll perceive that he speaks your language, that he inhabits your world of thought and feeling, that he belongs, in a word, to your nation – that great and terrible nation, which I love and fear and hate, the nation of Youth. In the end, of course, you'll leave the foreigner for the compatriot. But not before you've inflicted a good deal of suffering on everyone concerned, including yourself. And meanwhile, what about me? Shall I be still there for you to leave? Who knows? Not I, at any rate. I can no more answer for my future desires than for the Shah of Persia. For my future affection, yes. But it may last (how often, alas, affections do last that way!) only on condition of its object being absent. There are so many friends whom one's fond of when they're not there. Will you be one of them? It's the more possible since, after all, you're just as alien to me as I am to you. My country's called Middle-Ageia and everyone who was out of the egg of childhood before 1914 is my compatriot. Through all my desires, shouldn't I also pine to hear my own language, to speak with those who share the national traditions? Of course. But the tragedy of middle-aged life is that its army of banners is hardly ever captained by a compatriot. Passion is divorced from understanding, and the ageing man's desire attaches itself with an almost insane violence to precisely those outrageously fresh young bodies that house the most alien souls. Conversely, for the body of an understood and understanding soul, he seldom feels desire. And now, Pamela, suppose that my sentiment of your alienness should come to be stronger (as some time it must) than my desire for the lovely scandal of your young body. What then? This time I can answer; for I am answering for a self that changes very little through every change of circumstance – the self that doesn't intend to put up with more discomfort than it can possibly avoid; the self that, as the Freudians tell us, is homesick for that earthly paradise from which we've all been banished, our mother's womb, the only place on earth where man is genuinely omnipotent, where his every desire is satisfied, where he is perfectly at home and adapted to his surroundings, and therefore perfectly happy. Out of the womb we're in an unfriendly world, in which our wishes aren't anticipated, where we're no longer magically omnipotent, where we don't fit, where we're not snugly at home. What's to be done in this world? Either face out the reality, fight with it, resignedly or heroically accept to suffer or struggle. Or else flee. In practice even the strongest heroes do a bit of fleeing – away from responsibility into deliberate ignorance, away from uncomfort-able fact into imagination. Even the strongest. And conversely even the weakest fleers can make themselves strong. No, not the weakest; that's a mistake. The weakest become daydreamers, masturbators, paranoiacs. The strong fleer is one who starts with considerable advantages. Take my case. I'm so endowed by nature that I can have a great many of the prizes of life for the asking – success, money in reasonable quantities, love. In other words, I'm not entirely out of the womb; I can still, even in the extra-uterine world, have at least some of my desires magically satisfied. To have my wishes fulfilled I don't have to rush off every time to some imaginary womb-substitute. I have the power to construct a womb for myself out of the materials of the real world. But of course it's not a completely perfect and watertight womb; no post-natal uterus can ever in the nature of things be that. It lets in a lot of unpleasantness and alienness and obstruction to wishes. Which I deal with by flight, systematic flight into unawareness, into deliberate ignorance, into irresponsibility. It's a weakness which is a source of strength. For when you can flee at will and with success (which is only possible if nature has granted you, as she has to me, the possibility of anarchic independence of society), what quantities of energy you save, what an enormous amount of emotional and mental wear and tear is spared you? I flee from business by leaving all my affairs in the hands of lawyers and agents, I flee from criticism (both the humiliations of misplaced and wrongly motivated praise and from the pain of even the most contemptible vermin's blame) by simply not reading what anybody writes of me. I flee from time by living as far as possible only in and for the present. I flee from cold weather by taking the train or ship to places where it's warm. And from women I don't love anymore, I flee by just silently vanishing. For, like Palmerston, I never explain and never apologise. I just fade out. I decline to admit their existence. I consign their letters to the waste-paper basket, along with the press cuttings. Simple, crude even, but incredibly effective, if one's ready to be ruthless in one's weakness, as I am. Yes, quite ruthless, Pamela. If my desire grew weary or I felt homesick for the company of my compatriots, I'd just run away, determinedly, however painfully much you might still be in love with me, or your imagination, or your own hurt pride and humiliated self-love. And you, I fancy, would have as little mercy on my desires if they should happen to outlive what you imagine to be your passion for me. So that our love affair, if we were fools enough to embark on it, would be a race towards a series of successive goals – a race through boredom, misunderstanding, disillusion, towards the final winning-post of cruelty and betrayal. Which of us is likely to win the race? The betting, I should say, is about even, with a slight tendency in favour of myself. But there's not going to be a winner or a loser, for the good reason that there's not going to be any race. I'm too fond of you, Pamela, to…'

'Miles!' Fanning started so violently that a drop of ink was jerked from his pen on to the paper. He felt as though his heart had fallen into an awful gulf of emptiness. 'Miles!' He looked round. Two hands were clutching the bars of the unshuttered window and, as though desperately essaying to emerge from a subterranean captivity, the upper part of a face was peering in, over the high sill, with wide unhappy eyes.

'But Pamela!' There was reproach in his astonishment.

It was to the implied rebuke that she penitently answered. 'I couldn't help it, Miles,' she said; and, behind the bars, he saw her reddened eyes suddenly brighten and overflow with tears. 'I simply had to come.' Her voice trembled on the verge of breaking. '*Had* to.'

The tears, her words and that unhappy voice were moving. But he didn't want to be moved, he was angry with himself for feeling the emotion, with her for inspiring it. 'But, my dear child!' he began, and the reproach in his voice had shrilled to a kind of exasperation – the exasperation of one who feels himself hemmed in and helpless, increasingly helpless, against circumstances. 'But I thought we'd settled,' he began and broke off. He rose, and walked agitatedly towards the fireplace, agitatedly back again, like a beast in a cage; he was caught, hemmed in between those tearful eyes behind the bars and his own pity, with all those dangerous feelings that have their root in pity. 'I thought…' he began once more.

But, 'Oh!' came her sharp cry, and looking again towards the window he saw that only the two small hands and a pair of straining wrists were visible. The tragical face had vanished.

'Pamela?'

'It's all right.' Her voice came rather muffled and remote. 'I slipped. I was standing on a little kind of ledge affair. The window's so high from the ground,' she added plaintively.

'My poor child!' he said on a little laugh of amused commiseration. The reproach, the exasperation had gone out of his voice. He was conquered by the comic patheticness of her. Hanging on to the bars with those small, those rather red and childishly untended hands! And tumbling off the perch she had had to climb on, because the window was so high from the ground! A wave of sentimentality submerged him.

'I'll come and open the door.' He ran into the hall. Waiting outside in the darkness, she heard the bolts being shot back, one by one. Clank, clank! and then 'Damn!' came his voice from the other side of the door. 'These things are so stiff.... I'm barricaded up as though I were in a safe.' She stood there waiting. The door shook as he tugged at the recalcitrant bolt. The waiting seemed interminable. And all at once a huge, black weariness settled on her. The energy of wrought-up despair deserted her and she was left empty of everything but a tired misery. What was the good, what was the good of coming like this to be turned away again? For he *would* turn her away; he didn't want her. What was the good of renewing suffering, of once more dying?

'Hell and Death!' On the other side of the door Fanning was cursing like an Elizabethan. Hell and Death. The words reverberated in Pamela's mind. The pains of Hell, the darkness and dissolution of Death. What was the good? Clank! Another bolt had gone back. 'Thank goodness. We're almost...' A chain rattled. At the sound, Pamela turned and ran in a blind terror down the dimly lighted street.

'At last!' The door swung back and Fanning stepped out. But the sentimental tenderness of his outstretched hands wasted itself on empty night. Twenty yards away a pair of pale legs twinkled in the darkness.

'Pamela!' he called in astonishment. 'What the devil...?' The wasting on emptiness of his feelings had startled him into annoyance. He felt like one who has put forth all his strength to strike something and, missing his aim, swipes the unresisting air, grotesquely.

'Pamela!' he called again, yet louder. She did not turn at the sound of his voice, but ran on. These wretched high-heeled shoes! 'Pamela!' And then came the sound of his pursuing footsteps. She tried to run faster. But the pursuing footsteps came nearer and nearer. It was no good. Nothing was any good. She slackened her speed to a walk. 'But what on earth?' he asked from just behind her, almost angrily. Pursuing, he had called up within him the soul of a pursuer, angry and desirous. 'What on earth?' And suddenly his hand was on her shoulder. She trembled a little at the touch. 'But why?' he insisted. 'Why do you suddenly run away?'

But Pamela only shook her averted head. She wouldn't speak, wouldn't meet his eyes. Fanning looked down at her intently, questioningly. Why? And as he looked at the weary, hopeless face, he began to divine the reason. The anger of the pursuit subsided in him. Respecting her dumb, averted misery, he too was silent. He drew her comfortingly towards him. His arm around her shoulders, Pamela suffered herself to be led back towards the house.

Which would be best, he was wondering with the surface of his mind: to telephone for a taxi to take her back to the hotel, or to see if he could make up a bed for her in one of the upstairs rooms? But in the depths of his being he knew quite well that he would do neither of these things. He knew that he would be her lover. And yet, in spite of this deep knowledge, the surface mind still continued to discuss its little problems of cabs and bed-linen. Discussed it sensibly, discussed it dutifully. Because it would be a madness, he told himself, a criminal madness if he didn't send for the taxi or prepare that upstairs room. But the dark certainty of the depths rose suddenly and exploded at the surface in a bubble of ironic laughter, in a brutal and cynical world.

'Comedian!' he said to himself, to the self that agitatedly thought of telephones and taxis and pillow-slips. 'Seeing that it's obvious I'm going to have her.'

And, rising from the depths, her nakedness presented itself to him palpably in an integral and immediate contract with his whole being. But this was shameful, shameful. He pushed the naked Anadyomene back into the depths.[15] Very well, then (his surface mind resumed its busy efficient rattle), seeing that it was perhaps rather late to start telephoning for taxis, he'd rig up one of the rooms on the first floor. But if he couldn't find any sheets...? But here was the house, the open door.

Pamela stepped across the threshold. The hall was almost dark. Through a curtained doorway on the left issued a thin blade of yellow light. Passive in her tired misery, she waited. Behind her the chain rattled, as it had rattled only a few moments before, when she had fled from the ominous sound, and clank, clank! the bolts were thrust back into place.

'There,' said Fanning's voice. 'And now...' With a click, the darkness yielded suddenly to a brilliant light. Pamela uttered a little cry and covered her face with her hands. 'Oh, please,' she begged, 'please.' The light hurt her, was a sort of outrage. She didn't want to see, couldn't bear to be seen.

'I'm sorry,' he said, and the comforting darkness returned. 'This way.' Taking her arm he led her towards the lighted doorway on the left.

'Shut your eyes,' he commanded, as they approached the curtain. 'We've got to go into the light again; but I'll turn it out the moment I can get to the switch. Now!'

She shut her eyes and suddenly, as the curtain rings rattled, she saw, through her closed eyelids, the red shining of transparent blood. Still holding her arm, he led her forward into the room.

Pamela lifted her free hand to her face. 'Please don't look at me,' she whispered. 'I don't want you to see me like this. I mean, I couldn't bear...' Her voice faded to silence.

'I won't look,' he assured her. 'And anyhow,' he added, when they had taken two or three more steps across the room, 'now I can't.' And he turned the switch.

The pale translucent red went black again before her eyes. Pamela sighed. 'I'm so tired,' she whispered. Her eyes were still shut; she was too tired to open them.

'Take off your coat.' A hand pulled at her sleeve. First one bare arm, then the other, slipped out into the coolness.

Fanning threw the coat over a chair. Turning back, he could see her, by the tempered darkness that entered through the window, standing motionless before him, passive, wearily waiting, her face, her limp arms pale against the shadowy blackness.

'Poor Pamela,' she heard him say, and then suddenly light fingertips were sliding in a moth-winged caress along her arm. 'You'd better lie down and rest.'

The hand closed round her arm, she was pushed gently forward. That taxi, he was still thinking, the upstairs room... But his fingers preserved the silky memory of her skin, the flesh of her arm was warm and firm against his palm. In the darkness, the supernatural world was coming mysteriously, thrillingly into existence; he was once more standing upon its threshold.

'There, sit down,' came his voice. She obeyed; a low divan received her. 'Lean back.' She let herself fall on to pillows. Her feet were lifted on to the couch. She lay quite still. 'As though

I were dead,' she thought. She was unaware, through the darkness of her closed eyes, of his warm breathing presence, impending and very near. 'As though I were dead,' she inwardly repeated with a kind of pleasure. For the pain of her misery had ebbed away into the warm darkness, and to be tired, she found, to be utterly tired and to lie there utterly still were pleasures. 'As though I were dead.' And the light reiterated touch of his fingertips along her arm – what were those caresses but another mode, a soothing and delicious mode, of gently dying?

In the morning, on his way to the kitchen to prepare their coffee, Fanning caught sight of his littered writing table. He halted to collect the scattered sheets. Waiting for the water to boil, he read. 'By the time you receive this letter, I shall be – no, not dead, Pamela...' He crumpled up each page as he had finished reading it and threw it into the dustbin.

9

The architectural background was like something out of Alma Tadema. But the figures that moved across the sunlit atrium, that lingered beneath the colonnades and in the coloured shadow of the awnings, the figures were Hogarthian and Rowlandsonian, were the ferocious satires of Daumier and Rouveyre. Huge jellied females overflowed the chairs on which they sat. Sagging and with the gait of gorged bears, old men went slowly shambling down the porticoes. Like princes preceded by their outriders, the rich fat burgesses strutted with dignity behind their bellies. There was a hungry prowling of gaunt emaciated men and women, yellow-skinned and with tragical, blue-injected eyes. And, conspicuous by their trailing blackness, these bloated or cadaverous pencillings from an anti-clerical notebook were priests.

In the midst of so many monsters Pamela was a lovely miracle of health and beauty. These three months had subtly transformed her. The rather wavering and intermittent *savoir-vivre*, the child's forced easiness of manner, had given place to a woman's certainty, to that repose even in action, that decision even in repose, which are the ordinary fruits of the intimate knowledge, the physical understanding of love.

'For it isn't only murder that will out,' as Fanning had remarked some few days after the evening of the fireworks. 'It isn't only murder. If you could see yourself, my child! It's almost indecent. Anyone could tell that you'd been in bed with your lover. Could tell in the dark, even; you're luminous, positively luminous. All shining and smooth and pearly with love-making. It's really an embarrassment to walk about with you. I've a good mind to make you wear a veil.'

She had laughed, delightedly. 'But I don't mind them seeing. I *want* them to see. I mean, why should one be ashamed of being happy?'

That had been three months since. At present she had no happiness to be ashamed of. It was by no shining of eyes, no luminous soft pearliness of smoothed and rounded contour that she now betrayed herself. All that her manner, her pose, her gestures proclaimed was the fact that there *had* been such shinings and pearly smoothings, once. As for the present, her shut and sullen face announced only that she was discontented with it and with the man who, sitting beside her, was the symbol and the embodiment of that unsatisfactory present. A rather sickly embodiment at the moment, a thin and jaundiced symbol. For Fanning was hollow-cheeked, his eyes darkly ringed, his skin pale and sallow under the yellowed tan. He was on his way to becoming one of those pump-room monsters at whom they were now looking, almost incredulously. For, 'Incredible!' was Fanning's comment. 'Didn't I tell you that they simply weren't to be believed?' Pamela shrugged her shoulders, almost imperceptibly, and did not answer. She did not feel like answering, she wanted to be uninterested, sullen, bored. 'How right old Butler was!' he went on, rousing himself by the stimulus of his own talk from the depression into which his liver and Pamela had plunged him. 'Making the Erewhonians punish illness as a crime – how right! Because they *are* criminals, all these people. Criminally ugly and deformed, criminally incapable of enjoyment. Look at them. It's a caution. And when I think that I'm one of them...' He shook his head.

'But let's hope this will make me a reformed character.' And he emptied, with a grimace of disgust, his glass of tepid salt water. 'Revolting! But I suppose it's right that Montecatini should be a place of punishment as well as cure. One can't be allowed to commit jaundice with impunity. I must go and get another glass of my punishment – my purgatory, in every sense of the word,' he added, smiling at his own joke. He rose to his feet painfully (every movement was now a painful effort to him) and left her, threading his way through the crowd where, behind their marble counters, the pump-room barmaids dispensed warm laxatives from rows of polished brass taps.

The animation had died out of Fanning's face as he turned away. No longer distracted and self-stimulated by talk, he relapsed at once into melancholy. Waiting his turn behind two bulging monsignori at the pump, he looked so gloomily wretched that a passing connoisseur of the waters pointed him out to his companion as a typical example of the hepatic pessimist. But bile, as a matter of fact, was not the only cause of Fanning's depression. There was also Pamela. And Pamela – he admitted it, though the fact belonged to that great class of humiliating phenomena whose existence we are always trying to ignore – Pamela, after all, was the cause of the bile. For if he had not been so extenuated by that crazy love-making in the narrow cells of the Passionist Fathers at Monte Cavo, he would never have taken chill and the chill would never have settled on his liver and turned to jaundice. As it was, however, that night of the full moon had finished him. They had gone out, groping their way through the terrors of the nocturnal woods, to a little grassy terrace among the bushes, from which there was a view of Nemi. Deep sunk in its socket of impenetrable darkness and more than half eclipsed by shadow, the eye of water gleamed up at them secretly, as though through eyelids almost closed. Under the brightness of the moon, the hills, the woods seemed to be struggling out of ghostly greyness towards colour, towards the warmth of life. They had sat there for a while, in silence, looking. Then, taking her in his arms, '*Ceda al tatto la vista, al labro il lume*'[16] he had quoted with a kind of mockery – mocking her for the surrender to which he knew he could bring her, even against her will, even though, as he could see, she had made up her mind to sulk at him, mocking himself at the same time for the folly which drove him, weary and undesiring, to make the gesture. '*Al labro il lume*', he repeated with that undercurrent of derision in his voice, and leaned towards her. Desire returned to him as he touched her, and with it a kind of exultation, a renewal (temporary, he knew, and illusory) of all his energies.

'No, Miles. Don't. I don't want...' And she had averted her face, for she was angry, resentful, she wanted to sulk. Fanning knew it, mockingly, and mockingly he turned back her face towards him – '*al labro il lume*' – and found her lips. She struggled a little in his arms, protested, and then was silent, lay still. His kisses had had the power to transform her. She was another person, different from the one who had sulked and been resentful. Or rather she was two people – the sulky and resentful one, with another person superimposed, a person who quiveringly sank and melted under his kisses, melted and sank down, down towards that mystical death, that apocalypse, that almost terrible transfiguration. But beneath, to one side, stood always the angry sulker, unappeased, unreconciled, ready to emerge again (full of a new resentment for the way she had been undignifiedly hustled off the stage) the moment the other should have retired. His realisation of this made Fanning all the more perversely ardent, quickened the folly of his passion with a kind of derisive hostility. He drew his lips across her cheek, and suddenly their soft electrical touch on her ear made her shudder. 'Don't!' she implored, dreading and yet desiring what was to come. Gently, inexorably his teeth closed, and the petal of cartilage was a firm elastic resistance between them. She shuddered yet more violently. Fanning relaxed the muscles of his jaws, then tightened them once more, gently, against that exquisite resistance. The felt beauty of rounded warmth and resilience was under his hand. In the darkness they were inhabitants of the supernatural world.

But at midnight they found themselves, almost suddenly, on earth again, shiveringly cold under the moon. Cold, cold to the quick, Fanning had picked himself up. They stumbled homewards through the woods, in silence. It was in a kind of trance of chilled and sickened exhaustion that he had at last dropped down on his bed in the convent cell. Next morning he was ill. The liver was always his weak point. That had been nearly three weeks ago.

The second of the two monsignori moved away; Fanning stepped into his place. The barmaid handed him his hot dilute sulphate of soda. He deposited fifty centesmi as a largesse and walked off, meditatively sipping. But returning to the place from which he had come, he found their chairs occupied by a pair of obese Milanese businessmen. Pamela had gone. He explored the Alma Tadema background; but there was no sign of her. She had evidently gone back to the hotel. Fanning, who still had five more glasses of water to get through, took his place among the monsters round the bandstand.

In her room at the hotel Pamela was writing up her diary.

'September 20th. Montecatini seems a beastly sort of hole, particularly if you come to a wretched little hotel like this, which M. insisted on doing, because he knows the proprietor, who is an old drunkard and also cooks the meals, and M. has long talks with him and says he's like a character in Shakespeare, which is all very well, but I'd prefer better food and a room with a bath, not to mention the awfulness of the other people in the hotel, one of whom is the chief undertaker in Florence, who's always boasting to the other people at meal times about his business and what a fine motor hearse with gilded angels he's got and the number of counts and dukes he's buried. M. had a long conversation with him and the old drunkard after dinner yesterday evening about how you pre-serve corpses on ice and the way to make money by buying up the best sites at the cemetery and holding them till you could ask five times as much as you paid, and it was the first time I'd seen him looking cheerful and amused since his illness and even for some time before, but I was so horrified that I went off to bed. This morning at eight to the pump-room, where M. has to drink eight glasses of different kinds of water before breakfast and there are hundreds of hideous people all carrying mugs, and huge fountains of purgatives, and a band playing the 'Geisha', so I came away after half an hour, leaving M. to his waters, because I really can't be expected to watch him drinking, and it appears there are six hundred WCs.'

She laid down her pen and, turning round in her chair, sat for some time pensively staring at her own reflection in the wardrobe mirror.

'If you look long enough' (she heard Clare's voice, she saw Clare, inwardly, sitting at her dressing table), 'you begin to wonder if it isn't somebody else. And perhaps, after all, one *is* somebody else, all the time.' Somebody else, Pamela repeated to herself, somebody else. But was that a spot on her cheek, or a mosquito bite? A mosquito, thank goodness. 'Oh God,' she said aloud, and in the looking glass somebody else moved her lips, 'if only I knew what to do! If only I were dead!'

She touched wood hastily. Stupid to say such things. But if only one knew, one were certain! All at once she gave a little stiff sharp shudder of disgust, she grimaced as though she had bitten on something sour. 'Oh, oh!' she groaned; for she had suddenly seen herself in the act of dressing, there, in that moon-flecked darkness, among the bushes, that hateful night just before Miles fell ill. Furious because he'd humiliated her, hating him; she hadn't wanted to and he'd made her. Somebody else had enjoyed beyond the limits of enjoyment, had suffered a pleasure transmuted into its opposite. Or rather *she* had done the suffering. And then that further humiliation of having to ask him to help her to look for her suspender belt! And there were leaves in her hair. And when she got back to the hotel, she found a spider squashed against her skin under the chemise. Yes, *she* had found the spider, not somebody else.

Between the brackish sips Fanning was reading in his pocket edition of the *Paradiso*. '*L'acqua che prendo giammai non si corse*,'[16] he murmured.

> '*Minverva spira e conducemi Apollo,*
> *e nove Muse mi dimostran l'Orse.*'[18]

He closed his eyes. '*E nove Muse mi dimonstran l'Orse.*' What a marvel! 'And the nine Muses point me to the Bears.' Even translated the spell did not entirely lose its potency.

'How glad I shall be,' he thought, 'to be able to do a little work again.'

'*Il caffè?*' said a voice at his elbow. '*Non lo bevo mai, mai. Per il fegato, sa, è pessimo. Si dice anche che per gl'intestini…*'[19] The voice receded out of hearing.

Fanning took another gulp of salt water and resumed his reading.

> *Voi altri che drizzante il collo*
> *per tempo al pan degli angeli, del quale*
> *vivesi qui ma non sen vien satollo…*[20]

The voice had returned. '*Pesce bollito, carne ai ferri o arrostita, patate lesse…*'[21]

He shut his ears and continued. But when he came to,

> *La concreata e perpetua sete*
> *del deiforme regno,*[22]

he had to stop again. This craning for angels' bread, this thirsting for the god-like kingdom... The words reverberated questioningly in his mind. After all, why not? Particularly when man's bread made you sick (he thought with horror of that dreadful vomiting of bile), when it was a case of *pesce bollito* and you weren't allowed to thirst for anything more palatable than this stuff. (He swigged again.) These were the circumstances when Christianity became appropriate. Christians, according to Pascal, ought to live like sick men; conversely, sick men can hardly escape being Christians. How pleased Colin Judd would be! But the thought of Colin was depressing, if only all Christians were like Dante! But in that case, what a frightful world it would be! Frightful.

La concreata a perpetua sete
del deiforme regno cen portava
Veloci, quasi come il ciel vedete.
Beatrice in suso ed io in lei guardava...[23]

He thought of Pamela at the fireworks. On that pedestal. *Ben son, ben son Beatrice* on that pedestal. He remembered what he had said beneath the blossoming of the rockets; and also what he had meant to say about those legs which the pedestal made so easy for the worshipper to pinch. Those legs, how remote now, how utterly irrelevant! He finished off his third glass of Torretta and, rising, made his way to the bar for his first of Regina. 'Yes, how utterly irrelevant!' he thought. A complete solution of continuity. You were on the leg level, then you vomited bile, and as soon as you were able to think of anything but vomiting, you found yourself on the Dante level. He handed his mug to the barmaid. She rolled black eyes at him as she filled it. Some liverish gentlemen, it seemed, could still feel amorous. Or perhaps it was only the obese ones.

Fanning deposited his offering and retired. Irrelevant, irrelevant. It seemed, now, the unlikeliest story. And yet there it was, a fact. And Pamela was solid, too solid.

Phrases floated up, neat and ready-made, to the surface of his mind.

'What does he see in her? What on earth can she see in him?'

'But it's not a question of sight, it's a question of touch.'

And he remembered – *sentiments-centimètres* – that French pun about love, so appallingly cynical, so humiliatingly true. 'But only humiliating,' he assured himself, 'because we choose to think it so, arbitrarily, only cynical because *Beatrice in suso ed io in lei guardava*; only appalling because we're creatures who sometimes vomit bile and because, even without vomiting, we sometimes feel ourselves naturally Christians.' But in any case, '*nove Muse mi dimostran l'Orse*'. Meanwhile, however… He tilted another gill of water down his throat. And when he was well enough to work, wouldn't he also be well enough to thirst again for that other god-like kingdom, with its different ecstasies, its other peace beyond all understanding? But *tant mieux, tant mieux*, so long as the Bears remained unmoved and the Muses went on pointing.

Pamela was looking through her diary.

'June 24th,' she read. 'Spent the evening with M. and afterwards he said how lucky it was for me that I'd been seduced by him, which hurt my feelings (that word, I mean) and also rather annoyed me, so I said he certainly hadn't seduced me, and he said, all right, if I liked to say that I'd seduced him, he didn't mind, but anyhow it was lucky because almost anybody else wouldn't have been such a good psychologist as he, not to mention physiologist, and I should have hated it. But I said, how could he say such things? Because it wasn't that at all and I was happy because I loved him, but M. laughed and said, you don't, and I said, I do, and he said, you don't, but if it gives you any pleasure to imagine you do, imagine, which upset me still more, his not believing, which is due to his not wanting to love himself, because I *do love*...'

Pamela quickly turned the page. She couldn't read that sort of thing now.

'June 25th. Went to the Vatican where M...' She skipped nearly a page of Miles's remarks on classical art and the significance of orgies in the ancient religions; on the duty of being happy and having the sun inside you, like a bunch of ripe grapes; on making the world appear infinite and holy by an improvement of sensual enjoyment; on taking things untragically, unponderously.

'M. dined out and I spent the evening with Guy, the first time since the night of the fireworks, and he asked me what I'd been doing all this time, so I said, nothing in particular, but I felt myself blushing, and he said, anyhow you look extraordinarily well and happy and pretty, which also made me rather uncomfortable, because of what M. said the other day about murder will out, but then I laughed, because it was the only thing to do, and Guy asked what I was laughing about, so I said, nothing, but I could see by the way he looked at me that he was rather thrilled, which pleased me, and we had a very nice dinner and he told me about a girl he'd been in love with in Ireland and it seems they went camping together for a week, but he was never her lover because she had a kind of terror of being touched, but afterwards she went to America and got married. Later on, in the taxi, he took my hand and even tried to kiss me, but I laughed, because it was somehow very funny, I don't know why, but afterwards, when he persisted, I got very angry with him.

'June 27th. Went to look at mosaics today, rather fine, but what a pity they're all in churches and always pictures of Jesus and sheep and apostles and so forth. On the way home we passed a wine shop and M. went in and ordered a dozen bottles of champagne, because he said that love can exist without passion, or understanding, or respect, but not without champagne. So I asked him if he really loved me, and he said, *Je t'adore*, in French, but I said, no, do you really *love* me? But he said, silence is golden and it's better to use one's mouth for kissing and drinking champagne and eating caviar, because he'd also bought some caviar; and if you start talking about love and thinking about love, you get everything wrong, because it's not *meant* to be talked about, but acted, and if people want to talk and think, they'd better talk about mosaics and that sort of thing. But I still went on asking him if he loved me...'

'Fool, fool!' said Pamela aloud. She was ashamed of herself. Dithering on like that! At any rate Miles had been honest; she had to admit that. He'd taken care to keep the thing on the champagne level. And he'd always told her that she was imagining it all. Which had been intolerable, of course; he'd been wrong to be so right. She remembered how she had cried when he refused to answer her insistent question; had cried and afterwards allowed herself to be consoled. They went back to his house for supper; he opened a bottle of champagne, they ate the caviar. Next day he sent her that poem. It had arrived at the same time as some flowers from Guy. She reopened her notebook. Here it was.

At the red fountain's core the thud of drums
Quickens; for hairy-footed moths explore
This aviary of nerves; the woken birds
Flutter and cry in the branched blood; a bee
Hums with his million-times-repeated stroke
On lips your breast promotes geometers
To measure curves, to take the height of mountains,

The depth and silken slant of dells unseen.
I read your youth, as the blind student spells
With finger-tips the song from Cymbeline.
Caressing and caressed, my hands perceive
(In lieu of eyes) old Titian's paradise
With Eve unaproned; and the Maja dressed
Whisks off her muslins, that my skin may know
The blind night's beauty of brooding heat and cool,
Of silk and fibre, of molten-moist and dry,
Resistance and resilience.
But the drum
Throbs with yet faster beat, the wild birds go
Through their red liquid sky with wings yet more
Frantic and yet more desperate crying. Come!
The magical door its soft and breathing valves
Has set ajar. Beyond the threshold lie
Worlds after worlds receding into light,
As rare old wines on the ravished tongue renew
A miracle that deepens, that expands,
Blossoms, and changes hue, and chimes, and shines.
Birds in the blood and doubled drums incite
Us to the conquest of these new, strange lands
Beyond the threshold, where all common times,
Things, places, thoughts, events expire, and life
Enters eternity.

The darkness stirs, the trees are wet with rain;
Knock and it shall be opened, oh, again,
Again! The child is eager for its dam
And I the mother am of thirsty lips,
Oh, knock again!
Wild darkness wets this sound of strings.
How smooth it slides among the clarinets,

How easily slips through the trumpetings!
Sound glides through sound, and lo! the apocalypse,
The burst of wings above a sunlit sea.
Must this eternal music make an end?
Prolong, prolong these all but final chords!
Oh, wounded sevenths, breathlessly suspend
Our fear of dying, our desire to know
The song's last words!
Almost Bethesda sleeps, uneasily.
A bubble domes the flatness; gyre on gyre,
The waves expand, expire, as in the deeps
The woken spring subsides
Play, music, play!
Reckless of death, a singing giant rides
His storm of music, rides; and suddenly
The tremulous mirror of the moon is broken;
On the furthest beaches of our soul, our flesh,
The tides of pleasure foaming into pain
Mount, hugely mount; break; and retire again.
The final word is sung, the last word spoken.

'Do I like it, or do I rather hate it? I don't know.'

'June 28th. When I saw M. at lunch today, I told him I didn't really know if I liked his poem, I mean apart from literature, and he said, yes, perhaps the young *are* more romantic than they think, which rather annoyed me, because I believe he imagined I was shocked, which is too ridiculous. All the same, I *don't* like it.'

Pamela sighed and shut her eyes, so as to be able to think more privately, without distractions. From this distance of time she could see all that had happened in perspective, as it were, and as a whole. It was her pride, she could see, her fear of looking ridiculously romantic that had changed the quality of her feelings towards Miles – a pride and a fear on which he had played, deliberately. She had given herself with passion and desperately, tragically, as she imagined that Joan would have desperately given herself, at first sight, to a reluctant Walter. But the love he had offered her in return was a thing of laughter and frank, admitted sensuality, was a gay and easy companionship enriched, but uncomplicated, by pleasure. From the first he had refused to come up to her emotional level. From the first he had taken it for granted – and his taking it for granted was in itself an act of moral compulsion – that she should descend to his. And she had descended – reluctantly at first, but afterwards without a struggle. For she came to realise, almost suddenly, that after all she didn't really love him in the tragically passionate way she had supposed she loved him. In a propitious emotional climate her belief that she was a despairing Joan might perhaps have survived, at any rate for a time. But it was such a hot-house growth of the imagination; in the cool dry air of his laughter and cheerfully cynical frankness it had withered.

And all at once she had found herself, not satisfied, indeed, with what he offered, but superficially content. She returned him what he gave. Less even than he gave. For soon it became apparent to her that their *rôles* were being reversed, that the desperate one was no longer herself, but Miles. For 'desperate' – that was the only word to describe the quality of his desires. From light and gay – and perhaps, she thought, the lightness had been forced, the gaiety fabricated for the occasion as a defence against the tragical vehemence of her attack and of his own desires – his sensuality had become heavy, serious, intense. She had found herself the object of a kind of focused rage. It had been frightening sometimes, frightening and rather humiliating; for she had often felt that, so far as he was concerned, she wasn't there at all; that the body between those strong, those ruthless and yet delicate, erudite, subtly intelligent hands of his, that were like a surgeon's or a sculptor's hands, was not her body, was no one's body, indeed, but a kind of abstraction, tangible, yes, desperately tangible, but still an abstraction. She would have liked to rebel; but the surgeon was a master of his craft, the sculptor's fingers were delicately learned and intelligent. He had the art to overcome her reluctances, to infect her with some of his strange, concentrated seriousness. Against her will. In the intervals he resumed his old manner; but the laughter was apt to be bitter and spiteful, there was a mocking brutality in the frankness.

Pamela squeezed her eyes more tightly shut and shook her head, frowning at her memories. For distraction she turned back to her diary.

'June 30th. Lunched with Guy, who was really rather tiresome, because what is more boring than somebody being in love with you, when you're not in love with them? Which I told him quite frankly, and I could see he was dreadfully upset, but what was I to do?'

Poor Guy! she thought, and she was indignant, not with herself, but with Fanning. She turned over several pages. It was July now and they were at Ostia for the bathing. It was at Ostia that that desperate seriousness had come into his desire. The long hot hours of the siesta were propitious to his earnest madness. Propitious also to his talents, for he worked well in the heat. Behind her lowered eyelids Pamela had a vision of him sitting at his table, stripped to a pair of shorts, sitting there, pen in hand, in the next room and with an open door between them, but somehow at an infinite distance. Terrifyingly remote, a stranger more foreign for being known so well, the inhabitant of other worlds to which she had no access. They were worlds which she was already beginning to hate. His books were splendid, of course; still, it wasn't much fun being with a man who, for half the time, wasn't there at all. She saw him sitting there, a beautiful naked stranger, brown and wiry, with a face like brown marble, stonily focused on his paper.

And then suddenly this stranger rose and came towards her through the door, across the room. 'Well?' she heard herself saying. But the stranger did not answer. Sitting down on the edge of her bed, he took the sewing out of her hands and threw it aside on to the dressing table. She tried to protest, but he laid a hand on her mouth. Wordlessly he shook his head. Then, uncovering her mouth, he kissed her. Under his surgeon's, his sculptor's hands, her body was moulded to a symbol of pleasure. His face was focused and intent, but not on her, on something else, and serious, serious like a martyr's, like a mathematician's, like a criminal's. An hour later he was back at his table in the next room, in the next world, remote, a stranger once again – but he had never ceased to be a stranger.

Pamela turned over two or three more pages. On July 12th they went sailing and she had felt sick; Miles had been provokingly well at the time. The whole of the sixteenth had been spent in Rome. On the nineteenth they drove to Cerveteri to see the Etruscan tombs. She had been furious with him, because he had put out the lamp and made horrible noises in the cold sepulchral darkness, underground – furious with terror, for she hated the dark.

Impatiently Pamela went on turning the pages. There was no point in reading; none of the really important things were recorded. Of the earnest madness of his love-making, of those hands, that reluctantly suffered pleasure she hadn't been able to bring herself to write. And yet those were the things that mattered. She remembered how she had tried to imagine that she was like her namesake of *Pastures New* – the fatal woman whose cool detachment gives her such power over her lovers. But the facts had proved too stubborn; it was simply impossible for her to pretend that this handsome fancy-picture was her portrait. The days flicked past under her thumb.

'July 30th. On the beach this morning we met some friends of M.'s, a journalist called Pedder, who has just come to Rome as correspondent for some paper or other, and his wife, rather awful, I thought, both of them, but M. seemed to be extraordinarily pleased to see them, and they bathed with us and afterwards came and had lunch at our hotel, which was rather boring so far as I was concerned, because they talked a lot about people I didn't know, and then there was a long discussion about politics and history and so forth, *too* highbrow, but what was intolerable was that the woman thought she ought to be kind and talk to me meanwhile about something I could understand, so she talked about shops in Rome and the best places for getting clothes, which was rather ridiculous, as she's obviously one of those absurd arty women, who appeared in M.'s novels as young girls just before and during the war, so advanced in those days, with extraordinary coloured stockings and frocks like pictures by Augustus John. Anyhow, what she was wearing at lunch was really too fancy-dress, and really at her age one ought to have a little more sense of the decencies, because she must have been quite thirty-five. So that the idea of talking about smart shops in Rome was quite ludicrous to start with, and anyhow it was so insulting to me, because it implied that I was too young and half-witted to be able to take an interest in their beastly conversation.

'But afterwards, apropos of some philosophical theory or other, M. began talking about his opium smoking, and he told them all the things he'd told me and a lot more besides, and it made me feel very uncomfortable and then miserable and rather angry, because I thought it was only me he talked to like that, so confidentially, but now I see he makes confidences to everybody and it's not a sign of his being particularly fond of a person, or in love with them, or anything like that. Which made me realise that I'm even less important to him than I thought, and I found I minded much more than I expected I should mind, because I thought I'd got past minding. But I *do* mind.'

Pamela shut her eyes again. 'I ought to have gone away then,' she said to herself. 'Gone straight away.' But instead of retiring, she had tried to come closer. Her resentment – for oh, how bitterly she resented those Pedders and his confidential manner towards them! – had quickened her love. She wanted to insist on being more specially favoured than a mere Pedder; and, loving him, she had the right to insist. By a process of imaginative incubation, she managed to revive some of the emotions she had felt before the night of the fireworks. Tragically, with a suicide's determination, she tried to force herself upon him. Fanning fought a retreating battle, ruthlessly. Oh, how cruel he could be, Pamela was thinking, how pitilessly cruel! The way he could shut himself up as though in an iron box of indifference! The way he could just fade out into absent silence, into another world! The way he could flutter out of an embarrassing emotional situation on the wings of some brilliant irrelevance! And the way he could flutter back again, the way he could compel you, with his charm, with the touch of his hands, to reopen the gates of your life to him, when you'd made up your mind to shut them against him for ever! And not content with forcing you to yield, he would mock you for your surrender, mock himself too for having attacked – jeering, but without seeming to jeer, indirectly, in some terrible little generalisation about the weakness of the human soul, the follies and insanities of the body. Yes, how cruel he could be! She reopened her eyes.

'August 10th. M. still very glum and depressed and silent, like a wall when I come near. I think he sometimes hates me for loving him. At lunch he said he'd got to go into Rome this afternoon, and he went and didn't come back till late, almost midnight. Waiting for him, I couldn't help crying.

'August 11th. Those Pedders came to lunch again today and all M.'s glumness vanished the moment he saw them and he was charming all through lunch and so amusing, that I couldn't help laughing, though I felt more like crying, because why should he be so much nicer and more *friendly* with them than with me? After lunch, when we went to rest, he came into my room and wanted to kiss me, but I wouldn't let him, because I said, I don't want to owe your fits of niceness to somebody else, and I asked him, why? why was he so much nicer to them than to me? And he said they were his people, they belonged to the same time as he did and meeting them was like meeting another Englishman in the middle of a crowd of Kaffirs in Africa. So I said, I suppose I'm the Kaffirs, and he laughed and said, no, not quite Kaffirs, not more than a Rotary Club dinner in Kansas City, with the Pedders playing the part of a man one had known at Balliol in 'ninety-nine. Which made me cry, and he sat on the edge of the bed and took my hand and said he was very sorry, but that's what life was like, and it couldn't be helped, because time was always time, but people weren't always the same people, but sometimes one person and sometimes another, sometimes Pedder-fanciers and sometimes Pamela-fanciers, and it wasn't my fault that I hadn't heard the first performance of *Pelléas* in 1902 and it wasn't Pedder's fault that he had, and therefore Pedder was his compatriot and I wasn't. But I said, after all, Miles, you're my lover, doesn't that make any difference? But he said, it's a question of speech, and bodies don't speak, only minds, and when two minds are of different ages it's hard for them to understand each other when they speak, but bodies can understand each other, because they don't talk, thank God, he said, because it's such a comfort to stop talking sometimes, to stop thinking and just *be*, for a change. But I said that might be all right for him, but just *being* was my ordinary life and the change for me was talking, was being friends with somebody who knew how to talk and do all the other things talking implies, and I'd imagined I was that, besides just being somebody he went to bed with, and that was why I was so miserable, because I found I wasn't, and those beastly Pedders were. But he said, damn the Pedders, damn the Pedders for making you cry! and he was so *divinely* sweet and gentle it was like gradually sinking, sinking and being drowned. But afterwards he began laughing again in that rather hurting way, and he said, your body's so much more beautiful than their minds – that is, so long as one's a Pamela-fancier; which I am, he said, or rather was and shall be, but now I must go and work, and he got up and went to his room, and I was wretched again.'

The entries of a few days later were dated from Monte Cavo. A superstitious belief in the genius of place had made Pamela insist on the change of quarters. They had been happy on Monte Cavo; perhaps they would be happy there again. And so, suddenly, the sea didn't suit her, she needed mountain air. But the genius of place is an unreliable deity. She had been as unhappy on the hilltop as by the sea. No, not quite so unhappy, perhaps. In the absence of the Pedders, the passion which their coming had renewed declined again. Perhaps it would have declined even if they had still been there. For the tissue of her imagination was, at the best of times, but a ragged curtain. Every now and then she came to a hole and through the hole she could see a fragment of reality, such as the bald and obvious fact that she didn't love Miles Fanning. True, after a peep through one of these indiscreet holes she felt it necessary to repent for having seen the facts, she would work herself up again into believing her fancies. But her faith was never entirely wholehearted. Under the superficial layer of imaginative suffering lay a fundamental and real indifference. Looking back now, from the further shore of his illness, Pamela felt astonished that she could have gone on obstinately imagining, in spite of those loopholes on reality, that she loved him. 'Because I didn't,' she said to herself, clear-sighted, weeks too late. 'I didn't.' But the belief that she did had continued, even on Monte Cavo, to envenom those genuinely painful wounds inflicted by him on her pride, her self-respect, inflicted with a strange malice that seemed to grow on him with the passage of days.

'August 23rd.' She had turned again to the notebook.

'M. gave me this at lunch today.

Sensual heat and sorrow cold
Are undivided twins;
For there where sorrow ends, consoled,
Lubricity begins.

'I told him I didn't exactly see what the point of it was, but I supposed it was meant to be hurting, because he's always trying to be hurting now, but he said, no, it was just a Great Thought for putting into Christmas crackers. But he did mean to hurt, and yet in one way he's crazy about me, he's...'

Yes, crazy was the right word. The more and the more crazily he had desired her, the more he had seemed to want to hurt her, to hurt himself too – for every wound he inflicted on her was inflicted at the same time on himself. 'Why on earth didn't I leave him?' she wondered as she allowed a few more days to flick past.

'August 29th. A letter this morning from Guy in Scotland, so no wonder he took such an endless time to answer mine, which is a relief in one way, because I was beginning to wonder if he wasn't answering on purpose, but also rather depressing, as he says he isn't coming back to Rome till after the middle of September and goodness knows what will have happened by that time. So I felt very melancholy all the morning, sitting under the big tree in front of the monastery, such a marvellous huge old tree with very bright bits of sky between the leaves and bits of sun on the ground and moving across my frock, so that the sadness somehow got mixed up with the loveliness, which it often does do in a queer way, I find. M. came out unexpectedly and suggested going for a little walk before lunch, and he was very sweet for a change, but I dare say it was because he'd worked well. And I said, do you remember the first time we came up to Monte Cavo? and we talked about that afternoon and what fun it had been, even the museum, I said, even my education, because the Apollo was lovely. But he shook his head and said *Apollo, Apollo, lama sabachthani*,[24] and when I asked why he thought his Apollo had abandoned him he said it was because of Jesus and the Devil, and you're the Devil, I'm afraid, and he laughed and kissed my hand, but I ought to wring your neck, he said. For something that's *your* fault, I said, because it's you who made me a Devil for yourself. But he said it was me who made him make me a Devil. So I asked how? And he said just by existing, just by having my particular shape, size, colour, and consistency, because if I'd looked like a beetle and felt like wood, I'd have never made him make me into a Devil. So I asked him why he didn't just go away, seeing that what was wrong with me was that I was there at all. But that's easier said than done, he said, because a Devil's one of the very few things you can't run away from. And I asked why not? And he said because you can't run away from yourself and a Devil is at least half you. Besides, he said, the essence of a vice is that it *is* a vice – it holds you. Unless it unscrews itself, I said, because I'd made up my mind that minute that I'd go away, and it was such a relief having made up my mind, that I wasn't furious or miserable any more, and when M. smiled and said, if it *can* unscrew itself, I just laughed.'

A little too early, she reflected, as she read the words; she had laughed too early. That night had been the night of the full moon (oh, the humiliation of that lost suspender belt, the horror of that spider squashed against her skin!) and the next day he had begun to be ill. It had been impossible, morally impossible to leave him while he was ill. But how ghastly illness was! She shuddered with horror. Ghastly! 'I'm sorry to be so repulsive,' he had said to her one day, and from her place at his bedside she had protested, but hypocritically, hypocritically. As Aunt Edith might have protested. Still, one's *got* to be hippo-ish, she excused herself, simply *got* to be sometimes.

'But, thank goodness,' she thought, 'he's better now.' In a day or two he'd be quite fit to look after himself. These waters were supposed to be miraculous.

She took a sheet of writing paper from the box on the table and uncorked the bottle of ink.

'Dear Guy,' she began, 'I wonder if you're back in Rome yet?'

Notes

1. The true art is to conceal art.

2. Great!

3. Fabulous!

4. From the perspective of eternity.

5. '*De mortuis nil nisi bonum dicendum est*': 'No evil is spoken of the dead.'

6. From a Neapolitan song by Vicenzo de Chiara: 'In close embrace, in close embrace, in love's ecstasy.'

7. With honourable intentions.

8. Who knows?

9. Sorrow in the family.

10. You are a pig.

11. '*Observe me well. I am, in sooth, I am/Beatrice*,' from Dante's *The Divine Comedy*, 'Purgatory', XXX. 73, translated by Henry Francis Cary (London: George Newnes, 1903).

12. At fifty one goes a little mad.

13. Mad and a pig. Yes, and I am becoming a pig. Minors, for fifty-year-olds are an obsession. Yes, a real obsession.

14. Mr Podsnap is an extremely pompous character in Dickens's *Our Mutual Friend*.

15. Venus Anadyomene, or Venus Rising from the Sea, is an iconic representation of Aphrodite.

16. From a sonnet by Scipione Errico (1592–1670): '*Let sight yield to touch, the light to the lip.*'

17. '*The way that I pass/never yet was run*,' Dante, 'Paradise', II. 7, tr. Cary.

18. '*Minerva breathes the gale,/Apollo guides me, and another Nine/To my rapt sight the arctic beams reveal*,' Dante, 'Paradise', II. 8–10, tr. Cary.

19. Coffee? I never drink it, never, it is bad for the liver. They also say for the intestines...

20. '*Ye other few, who have outstretch'd the neck/Timely for food of angels, on which here/They live, yet never know satiety*,' Dante, 'Paradise', II. 11–13, tr. Cary.

21. Boiled fish, meat grilled or roasted, boiled potatoes...

22. '*The increate perpetual thirst, that draws/Toward the realm of God's own form*,' Dante, 'Paradise', II. 21–22, tr. Cary.

23. '*The increate perpetual thirst, that draws
Toward the realm of God's own form, bore us
Swift almost as the heaven ye behold.
Beatrice upward gaz'd, and I on her...*'
– Dante, 'Paradise', II. 21–24, tr. Cary

24. Apollo, Apollo, why have you forsaken me?

Biographical note

Aldous Huxley was born into an illustrious family in Surrey in 1894. His father Leonard Huxley was a schoolmaster and author, and his mother Julia Arnold the founder of Prior's Field school, niece of Matthew Arnold and sister of Mrs Humphrey Ward. She died when Huxley was fourteen. As a youth Huxley was educated at Eton College, and went on to study English Literature at Balliol College, Oxford. After leaving university, Huxley held several jobs, including a teaching post at Eton, during which time he taught Stephen Runciman and Eric Blair, who would later assume the pen name George Orwell.

An illness in his teens having left him almost blind, during the First World War Huxley spent some time working at Garsington Manor, the estate near Oxford of Lady Ottoline Morrell of the Bloomsbury set. During this time he met many luminaries of the literary world, not least among whom D.H. Lawrence, who became a friend and whose letters he later edited.

Though his earlier literary efforts often took the form of poetry, Huxley began writing fiction in earnest during his early twenties and published his first novel, *Crome Yellow*, in 1921.

In 1937, Huxley moved to California with his first wife Maria Nys and their son Matthew. In America, Huxley wrote several Hollywood screenplays and gradually distanced himself from fiction, moving towards the essay as his preferred medium. He also became interested in spiritualism, exploring areas including Hindu philosophy and mysticism, and famously experimenting with drugs. He saw psychedelic drugs as a means of enlightenment, and his work *The Doors of Perception* (1954) was championed by youth movements in the 1960s and remains a cult favourite.

Huxley is now perhaps best known for works of futuristic fantasy: *Brave New World* (1932) and *The Island* (1962), are among the greatest works of twentieth-century literature.

Huxley was remarried in 1956, to violinist and psychotherapist Laura Archera. He died on 22nd November 1963, the day of John F. Kennedy's assassination.